MURDER IN LONDON

A 1950S COZY HISTORICAL MYSTERY

LEE STRAUSS
NORM STRAUSS

la plume
PRESS

Copyright © 2021 by Lee Strauss

Cover by Steven Novak

Cover Illustration by Amanda Sorenson

Library and Archives Canada Cataloguing in Publication

Title: Murder in London / Lee Strauss.

Names: Strauss, Lee (Novelist), author.

Description: Series statement: A Rosa Reed mystery ; 8 | "A 1950s cozy historical mystery".

Identifiers: Canadiana (print) 20210230800 | Canadiana (ebook) 20210230819 | ISBN 9781774091814

(hardcover) | ISBN 9781774091791 (softcover) | ISBN 9781774091807 (IngramSpark softcover) | ISBN

9781774091838 (Kindle) | ISBN 9781774091821 (EPUB)

Classification: LCC PS8637.T739 M879 2021 | DDC C813/.6—dc23

CHAPTER 1

$\mathcal{M}$iss Rosa Reed returned the telephone receiver to its cradle on the desk in the Forrester mansion study. Her breath hitched as she mentally replayed the conversation she had had with her mother, who lived in London, several time zones away from Rosa's new home in Santa Bonita, California. With her eyes closed, she inhaled deeply and exhaled slowly. If it hadn't already felt like her worlds were colliding with the unexpected arrival of her former fiancé, Lord Winston Eveleigh, this phone call had really brought the point home. Rosa's head felt dizzy from the juxtaposition.

In a near daze, she walked back to the dining room where a dinner party was underway. Along with the awkward addition of Winston were Rosa's family members, consisting of Aunt Louisa Forrester, Grandma Sally Hartigan, and her cousins Clarence and Gloria. Aunt Louisa's new gentleman friend, dude ranch operator Elliot Roundtree, and Rosa's boyfriend, Detective Miguel Belmonte, were also in attendance.

The room quieted when Rosa entered.

Aunt Louisa, who managed to eat without losing her lipstick, asked, "Is everything all right?"

Rosa, remaining poised, took her seat. Miguel's copper-brown eyes narrowed in concern, and he reached under the table for her hand and squeezed.

"I'm not sure," she answered, then looked across the table at Winston. "My parents have heard from the police. About Vivien. There's a new lead with Vivien's case."

Winston's face immediately drained of all expression. No one else spoke.

Elliot Roundtree, the one person at the table who'd never heard the name before, stroked his thick white mustache and asked innocently, "Who's Vivien?"

"Lady Vivien . . . my sister," Winston said, still staring at Rosa.

"She was my best friend," Rosa added.

Aunt Louisa, not seeing the need for tact, clarified. "She was murdered."

Mr. Roundtree, a rugged outdoor man who was rarely shaken, looked stunned. "Golly. Sorry to hear it."

"Almost six years ago," Rosa explained. "The case was never solved."

"A fresh break in the case?" Gloria said eagerly, pushing her short dark hair behind her ears. Seven years younger than Rosa, Gloria worked at a newspaper as a junior journalist and had a strong interest in Rosa's work as a private detective. The phrase "break in the case" was one of Gloria's favorite new expressions.

"I don't know all the details yet," Rosa said. "Apparently, they've captured a fugitive robber who they believe may be responsible for the crime."

Winston drank what remained in his wine glass then waved about for a servant that didn't exist. Rosa passed an open bottle to him, and he poured himself a generous portion. Then, holding the nearly empty bottle in the air, he said in his thick English accent, "Is anyone else interested?"

Clarence, who until this announcement had been enduring the dinner engagement with barely concealed boredom, held up his glass, and Winston emptied the bottle.

"As much as I regret it, I must cut my trip short," Winston said after another sip of wine. He gave Rosa a meaningful look. "I don't suppose you'd like to join me?"

Miguel's grip on Rosa's hand tightened.

With her free hand, she cupped Miguel's reassuringly. "I do plan on returning to London as soon as possible, but not as your companion, Winston." She turned to Miguel. "Would you'd like to come?"

Miguel's dark brows shot up in surprise. "To London?"

"We'll fly! You can do that nowadays, you know. It's how I traveled last time." She paused for a moment. "I know it's sudden."

Miguel smiled, and the dimples that Rosa simply adored appeared. "Absolutely," he said. "Delvecchio owes me some vacation time."

Winston abruptly pushed away from the table and whipped his cloth napkin onto it like a gauntlet. "I will see you in London, Rosa." He stormed out of the room, leaving everyone speechless.

Mr. Roundtree smirked. "Why do I have the feeling there's more to this story than meets the eye?"

Aunt Louisa folded her arms, having given up on the rest of her meal. "I'll tell you about it someday, Elliot." She steadied her gaze on Rosa. "It has all the elements of a Perry Mason novel."

The following day, Rosa, Gloria, and Aunt Louisa stood looking down at Diego, Rosa's brown tabby cat, who was curled up on the blue Scandinavian-style living room sofa. Aunt Louisa presented herself in a powder-blue dress with capped sleeves, a thin matching belt which emphasized her narrow waist, and a dramatically printed skirt, extra full thanks to the two or more crinoline slips underneath. But her face expressed doubt. Her arms crossed, and her foot tapped in annoyance.

Diego stared innocently up at them, his green-yellow eyes blinking slowly, as if he had a heart full of good intentions.

There wasn't one person in the room who believed that to be true.

"Are you sure you can't take him with you?" Aunt Louisa said.

Rosa shook her head. "I'm afraid not. The long journey would be very hard on him, and it would complicate matters."

"It's not exactly uncomplicated leaving him here," Aunt Louisa returned.

Rosa looked at her apologetically. Ever since she had brought the shivering and abandoned kitten home to the Forrester mansion, the tension between her aunt and the poor kitten had been evident. Then there was the incident with the imported drapes, the debacle with the expensive carpet in the library, and the scandal of the claw marks on the leather lounge chair. The list was extensive, and the cat unrepentant.

Even though "Deputy Diego," as Miguel liked to call him, had serendipitously helped to uncover evidence in several murder cases, his stock had not risen in Aunt Louisa's eyes. Grandma Sally *had* recently warmed to him somewhat, though. Rosa regarded this as miraculous, considering the numerous times the cat had startled the elderly lady by suddenly streaking through the living room, bounding on top of furniture, and knocking over plants in one of his trademark bursts of energy. One time, he had even knocked her reading glasses off while she attempted to read a book.

"He will be my responsibility," Gloria offered as she scooped his limp, furry form into her arms. "Diego loves me. And when I have to go to work at the paper, Señora Gomez will watch him."

As if on cue, the Forrester mansion's housekeeper and cook breezed past the open door, slowing when she registered the three women congregating. Her gaze settled on Diego in Gloria's arms. "Aww, look at him. *Es un ángelito.* A little angel!" She smiled at Diego before continuing to the kitchen.

Gloria buried her nose in the top of Diego's furry head as she spoke to Rosa. "I'll help you pack."

Rosa's bedroom had generous space with matching ornate wooden furniture and its *own* bathroom—something Rosa would miss when she was back at Hartigan House in South Kensington. Gloria placed Diego on the jade-green quilt and dramatically threw herself down on her back beside him. Rosa smiled. She knew that when Gloria offered to help pack, what she *really* meant was, "I'll lie on the bed and talk your ear off while I watch you work."

"You know, I don't leave until tomorrow after-noon," Rosa said. "I'm only going to pack a few things right now." Her suitcase lay open on the floor with a few sundry items in it.

"I wish I could go with you." Gloria sighed as she rolled onto her side to look at Rosa. "This place will be dullsville without you here."

"Well, I don't doubt that," Rosa returned cheerily,

"but I'm sure you'll manage to keep soldiering on without me for a little while."

Gloria rubbed the bridge of Diego's nose, a gesture that always caused him to close his eyes and calm down, if only for a few moments. "I don't know that much about Lady Vivien. Care to tell me more?"

Rosa lowered herself onto her vanity chair and regarded her image in the mirror. Like Gloria, she had short dark hair, curled stylishly at the nape of her neck. Though she'd taken after her father, Basil Reed, in looks, she'd gotten her mother's eyes, a striking green, and like her mother, did her best to choose dresses and makeup that brought them out. Rosa and Vivien had been opposites that way. Vivien had found fashion and society a challenge, prefer-ring reading and scribbling in her notebooks to social gatherings. As a Lady, her duties rarely allowed for such personal indulgences, and she often confessed to envying Rosa's freedom in that regard. It wasn't until Rosa had become engaged to Winston that she herself had felt the burden of social conven-tions to that degree.

"Vivien and I were the closest of friends since we were young girls. We shared a love for the law and a certain fascination with bringing those who broke the law to account. Though it was extremely unconventional, Vivien found her way to Birmingham to study law. Winston was livid and tried to prevent her from going to university, but, as she said, these were modern times, and men didn't own women anymore. Vivien had her own trust fund and could do what she wanted. Fortunately, Winston wasn't the type to hang around the house, and Vivien was free to come and go as she pleased without having to deal with his constant disdain."

"Seriously, Rosa," Gloria said. "You paint a grim picture of Winston. How did the two of you ever get to the point of engagement to be married?"

Rosa's shoulders fell. "Winston is older than Vivien and me by five years, and I'd created a romanticized version of him in my mind. He was older, dashing, and adventurous, or at least that's how he presented himself in those days. When he enlisted in the army, we both worried together if he was going to survive the fighting on the Western Front." Rosa watched Gloria in the reflection of the mirror, her youthful eyes bright with interest.

"As it turns out, he never was sent to the front, but he did look dashing in his uniform." Rosa sighed. "I confess to fantasizing about marrying him, more because he was Vivien's brother than from feelings of love. I wanted us to be sisters, if only by marriage."

Rosa twisted in her chair to face her cousin. "In my defense, I was only thirteen."

Gloria laughed. "Completely understandable."

Diego brushed against Rosa's leg, and she reached down to pull him onto her lap, where he instantly purred.

"Our emotional attachment didn't happen until after Vivien died. Our grief brought us together, and we found comfort in one another. Over time, we just settled into a friendship that, in hindsight, meant more to Winston than to me. He's the type of fellow who's used to getting what he wants. And he can be very persuasive. I think he just convinced me we should be married. We had such a comfortable friendship. I thought perhaps he was right."

Rosa gazed out the window at the palm trees swaying in the breeze; the Californian sun hung in the sky like a bright beacon. "I'd been in love before, and I didn't believe that could happen more than once in life, so I finally relented."

"Who did you love?"

Rosa looked at her cousin, who stared back at her, fists on her chin and eyes dreamy.

"Miguel."

"I know you love him now, but who did you love before?"

Rosa smiled. Gloria had only been a child when Rosa had lived with the Forrester family during World War Two. So she hadn't known about the forbidden love affair.

"Miguel. He was a soldier stationed in Santa Bonita. I was a senior in high school."

"Golly!" Gloria sat up so quickly, she startled Diego. Rosa "umphed" as the cat sprung off her lap and shot under the bed. Gloria continued undaunted. "That is the dreamiest thing I've ever heard. But, hey, did Mom know?"

"Not at first, and believe me, she wasn't happy when she did."

"Oh, Rosa. I can only imagine. But how romantic! And now he's going to London with you. No wonder Winston is so frosted."

They were interrupted by a soft knock on the door.

"Come in," Rosa called.

Bledsoe, the Forresters' butler, opened the door but was careful not to step into the room. "Lord Winston asked me to let you know he would like to talk to you right away."

Rosa shot Gloria a look. "Speak of the devil."

To Bledsoe, she said, "Please tell Lord Winston I'll be with him shortly."

Winston stood in the morning room, glancing out at the expansive Forrester mansion's backyard. He inhaled from his cigarette and exhaled a swirl of smoke. The kidney-shaped pool, three Mediterranean-style water fountains, and a tennis court were impressive, but the most eye-catching was the sparkling Pacific Ocean in the distance. He breathed in another puff and exhaled quickly. Rosa had mentioned she'd often enjoyed having her breakfast sitting poolside.

"I'm beginning to see why you've stayed here for so long," Winston said as Rosa entered the room. As usual, he was dressed casually but fashionably. This morning he wore a cardigan sweater over a white button-down shirt with a black tie and gray trousers. His hair, parted on one side, was held in place with a good portion of oil. Dotting his long, aristocratic nose were a few freckles, suggesting he'd spent some time at the pool. It was a profile Rosa had spent a lot of time looking at. While she, Gloria, and Clarence, who were all different shades of brunette and had similar features, Winston and Vivien had borne little resemblance to each other, with sharply contrasting complexions and hair color.

Rosa, in a very un-English sort of way, got straight to the point. "You wanted to talk to me?"

Winston glanced at her sideways with his penetrating blue eyes. "Yes, please." He gestured to one of the chairs at the empty table and sat down opposite it. "Am I right to assume that the reason you are eager to return to London is to take part in the investigation?"

"That's correct," Rosa said, refusing the proffered chair. Despite her sense of goodwill, she was rather enjoying the slight look of irritation on Winston's face at her defiance.

Winston crossed his legs and lit another cigarette. "I really wish you wouldn't."

"Why not?"

"I think this time you should just let the police manage my sister's murder investigation."

The unnecessarily possessive use of the words 'my sister' was not lost on Rosa.

"She was my best friend."

"Precisely why you should *not* get involved. You know what it did to you last time."

Rosa had gone through a wretched time of loss

and grief, which had manifested physically in weight loss and sleeplessness.

"I'm concerned about you," he pressed.

"Nonetheless, I'll be taking part. I'm sure the police will allow it." Rosa didn't like the defensiveness that had crept into her voice. "Besides, Miguel will be there and can offer an objective viewpoint."

Winston snorted derisively. "By gosh, Rosa. Your naivety astounds me. Do you think he's going to be any kind of help? It seems bringing your latest fling with you will only complicate matters."

"He's not a *fling!*"

"See here, I'm glad you're returning to London," he said, ignoring her protest. "In fact, I think it would be good for you to see your parents, perhaps visit some of your old haunts, renew your friendships, and so on, but to get entangled once again in all of this torrid affair . . ." He flicked long fingers in the air.

"You forget that I am a police officer—"

"You *were* a police officer," Winston corrected. "You left the force, did you not? Regardless, I can assure you that I'll be in close contact with the police the entire way, and I can keep you thoroughly updated as we go along. Besides, it's been a while since I visited Hartigan House, and I would be glad to see your parents again."

Rosa glared. How dare he minimize her talents and her capabilities. "I—"

"I want this murder solved as much as you do, Rosa." He stood and placed a warm palm on her arm. "Knowing Vivien's killer is still on the loose doing God knows what eats me up. He may even kill again for all we know." He whispered in her ear. "I'd hate anything to happen to you."

Rosa stepped back and pulled her arm free. "I can take care of myself, Winston."

He grinned. "You always were a fiery one. Still, I think it's best that you just trust me to take the lead on this, for your sake and the sake of my sister's memory."

Rosa gritted her teeth. Worried she'd say something she'd later regret, she didn't trust herself to speak at that moment.

"I managed to get a flight later tonight," Winston said. He nodded curtly and walked out of the room, pausing briefly to add, "I'll see you in London."

CHAPTER 2

*R*osa put her hand on Miguel's for the hundredth time to unclench his fingers from the armrest.

"Maybe you need to read a book or something," she said as she regarded the ashen tone of his creamed-coffee-brown cheeks. "The ones the stewardess offered us aren't exciting, but I have a few in my carry-on suitcase as well as some magazines."

"Maybe a magazine," Miguel muttered as he blew a slow breath through pursed lips.

Rosa thought for a moment. "Um, let's see. I have the January issue of *Vogue*. There's an article entitled 'Making an Asset of Your Shortcomings.' I think you might find it helpful."

"Very funny."

"Only joking. You have no shortcomings that I can think of."

"Love *is* blind, they say."

"Right. How about *Charm* magazine? Some great new hat fashions are coming out this spring."

"I'll pass."

"*Woman's Weekly?*"

Miguel scowled.

"Oh, I know! How about the latest issue of *Amigos with Ammo?* There's an entire section entitled 'Latino Men: Do They Really Make the Most Handsome Cops?' It's an opinion piece written by a blind woman named Esperanza." Rosa cleared her throat. "Unfortunately, there aren't any pictures."

For the first time since the plane had taken off from Los Angeles an hour earlier, Rosa detected a small smile tugging at the corners of Miguel's mouth.

"Now you're making stuff up." He turned to look out the window to hide his grin, but Rosa saw it.

Rosa thought he looked exceptionally handsome in his black suit and tie, slicked-back hair, and polished leather shoes. She'd rarely seen him dressed so formally, even in his role as a detective. Since he had never flown before, she had coached him a little in acceptable attire for flying.

She wore a pencil skirt to accommodate the narrow seating. She'd left her A-line skirts and dresses and her crinoline skirts behind, deciding packing light was more appropriate for the event. Instead, she'd packed slimmer dress cuts and long trousers. Besides, if Rosa needed to add to her wardrobe, she always had her mother's dress shop, Feathers & Flair, at her disposal.

"C'mon, hombre." She poked Miguel with her red-lacquered fingernail. "You can let go of the armrest. It's not going anywhere, and it might be nice to get some blood flowing in your fingers again."

Just then, a pretty blonde flight attendant came by with a tray, expertly balancing glasses of champagne.

Rosa accepted for them both. "Tonic for your nerves," she said to Miguel.

The flight attendant said, "Today's menu has a choice between prime rib and lobster."

Rosa chose lobster while Miguel took prime rib.

"Thank you, miss," he said.

"Aha. It takes a pretty flight attendant to relax your grip on the seat and get your stomach back on even ground."

"I think it was more the mention of prime rib."

He sipped the champagne and wrinkled his nose. "I'm more of a beer kind of guy."

Rosa pointed out of the window. "Is that Las Vegas down there?"

The sky was cloudless, and the landscape looked rugged and flat. The wing of the aircraft was just starting to obscure the view of a city far below.

"I think so."

"Enjoy the view now," Rosa said. "We have two stops: one in New York and then in Gander, Newfoundland. After that, there will be nothing but ocean below. It's a long trip. I should know—it's the same route I took flying over from London. Best to try and sleep as much as we can."

"I could have lived without the image of an endless ocean beneath this flying tin can."

"I do apologize. But people are flying across the ocean often these days. It might be something to get used to."

"I guess so." Miguel looked thoughtful. "You *have* told your parents about . . . you know . . . us, haven't you?" Miguel said. "They *do* know I'm coming along, right?"

"Well, I told them I would be bringing a colleague from the police department."

"A *colleague*?"

"Yes, it's true, isn't it? And I might've mentioned we're a little more than friends."

A shadow crossed Miguel's face.

Rosa patted his hand. "You'll be fine."

"How do you know? You've never brought someone like me home before. What if—"

"I haven't brought home many men in *any* case," Rosa said, interrupting. "And to answer your question, my parents will come to love you as I do."

For a few moments, Miguel grew suddenly quiet and stared out the window.

"Tell me more about the case," he said finally. "We've only talked about it in vague terms. What is waiting for us in London?"

"I haven't had a lot of detail from my mother yet, but yes, I need to tell you the details of the case, not that there are many." Rosa closed her eyes for a long moment. She'd given Gloria a summary of Vivien's case but hadn't spoken of the details of the actual murder with anyone since she'd fled the altar nearly a year ago. She dreaded the emotion she knew speaking of it would arouse, but she'd have to face it if Miguel was going to help investigate.

Miguel noticed her reticence. "It might be cathartic to talk about it."

Rosa grasped his hand in hers and l head on his shoulder. "I hope so."

He kissed her on the forehead, and summoned her courage.

"In 1951, Vivien was found strangled to death in Winston's private quarters at Kenway House, their family home in Knightsbridge. We were the same age, twenty-three. I was in my first year as a police constable. In celebration of my father's retirement, my parents were on an extended trip to North Africa. Because of his influence, I was allowed to be part of the investigation on a sort of 'unofficial' basis."

"What kind of place is Kenway House?"

Rosa sat up and leaned her head back on the seat. "Similar to Hartigan House where I grew up. It's a large four-story house. In England, by the way, the floors of a house are numbered differently than in America. What you would call the first floor, a Brit would call the ground floor, and then the next level would be the first floor."

"Good to know."

"Kenway House was built around 1840, I think. Winston and Vivien's parents died in a terrible car accident in 1948, and Winston and Vivien inherited everything. Being the firstborn and the only son, inston got the lion's share. Eventually, Winston had the whole first floor renovated to be his private quarters. He allocated the second floor to Vivien."

"They lived separately in the same house?"

"For all intents and purposes, yes. Of course, they had staff for cleaning and cooking, but they spent most of their time in the basement level where the kitchen is, or in their sleeping quarters in the attic."

Miguel whistled. "Sounds like a fairy-tale existence."

"Yes, but with a horrible ending for Vivien."

"How did they come by their wealth?" Miguel asked.

"Oh, it's old money. Queen Victoria made Winston's great-grandfather Eveleigh an earl. Winston has never had to work a day in his life."

"What theory did the police have at the time?"

"The most obvious one was that Vivien caught a thief trying to rob Winston's quarters. The poor woman was attacked and strangled. That was all we had to go on, but the police felt unsure about it. For one thing, it seemed that the perpetrator knew that Winston's private quarters occupied the first floor and knew exactly which window led to them. The thief climbed an iron trellis to get up to a window, which they broke to get in. It's an easy climb; anyone could have done it. I think they have now removed that trellis, of course. Secondly, the floor is quite large, but the killer ransacked almost every room. There were mirrors broken, books thrown off the shelves in the study, leather furniture slashed with a knife. Whoever did it could have had more on their mind than stealing some cash."

"Like what?"

"Possibly a vendetta against Winston or something, but nothing to prove that hypothesis materialized."

"What do you think?"

Rosa let out a long breath. "I've always thought it was someone who knew Winston rather than a random burglar. Someone familiar enough with the staff schedule to know they'd have gone for the night or be asleep in the attic where they wouldn't hear anything."

"Was it normal for Vivien to be in Winston's quarters?"

"Naturally, she passed the first-floor landing via the staircase on her way to the ground floor, but it wasn't her habit to enter Winston's rooms even when he was in residence. They weren't close like some siblings are. However, she certainly could have heard something suspicious and gone to investigate."

"What about the theory that Vivien was the target?"

"Of course, we entertained that idea, but we couldn't find any evidence that anybody had anything against Vivien."

"What about Winston?" Miguel asked, hardly concealing his distaste for the lord.

"He was at a hotel pub, The Baron's Goose, all night, celebrating a friend's birthday. Winston had too much to drink and opted to stay there for the night. The next morning, he went home, only to find that his sister had been killed. A neighbor, who happened to notice that a top window had been broken, had called the police."

"Fingerprints?"

"None except for Winston's, Vivien's, and members of staff. Nothing on the trellis outside, although there were footprints at the bottom and a few broken pieces of foliage on the way up. The window was broken inwards, but there were no fingerprints on the window frame or the glass."

Miguel hummed. "So, the killer wasn't only violent; he was meticulous."

"Exactly. He must have worn gloves. There was also a significant amount of cash missing."

"What about members of the staff at Kenway House?"

"No motives were found. All of them had solid alibis."

"Any other leads?"

"No, not really. Police arrested several criminals of note who were known for committing burglary. They all appeared to have decent alibis. A look into Winston's past relationships, lovers . . . didn't lead to anything solid. I spoke to several of Winston's friends who might have had various reasons for harboring animosity toward him. They all turned out to be dead-ends."

"Physical evidence?"

"Not a lot. The police found a folded piece of paper on Vivien's person with numbers scrawled in her handwriting, but we have no connection to anything. There were a few signs of a struggle. The killer was male due to the size of the bruises on her neck." Rosa paused. "I can't tell you how many times I have lain awake at night wishing I could grip the throat of Vivien's killer myself."

"Revenge is bitter sustenance."

"That's true," Rosa admitted. "Plato? Mark Twain?"

"Grandma Belmonte. She also told me to make

sure I paid back my older sister every time she did something to me, so . . ."

Rosa chuckled. "Did Carlotta pick on you a lot?"

"All the time, and to make matters worse, her friends Maria and Consuela used to come over and try to kiss me when I was seven. I'd get chased all around the yard."

"What a terrible childhood!"

"Traumatizing. To this day, Mexican women scare me a little."

"Aww, you poor man." Rosa raised their clasped hands to kiss his and then leaned back again. "Anyway, the police eventually stopped investigating. It was deemed a burglary gone wrong with the murderer still at large."

The stewardess arrived with their meals, and they were silent for a while as they enjoyed the surprisingly tasty fare.

Once their initial hunger pangs had abated, Miguel casually asked, "How did you and Winston end up together through all of this?"

Rosa lowered her fork and patted her mouth with the linen napkin provided. "It's long over with now. Do you really want to know?"

Miguel nodded and raised a brow. "It's better than reading *Amigos with Ammo*."

"Very well." Rosa took a deep breath. "Lord and Lady Eveleigh and my parents were acquaintances with overlapping social circles, so Vivien and I played together as little girls. Then we went to the same boarding school and got very close. After I got back from America, her parents died. I spent a lot of time with her to help her get through that. After her death, Winston swooped in and let me lean on him for strength. It was a very vulnerable time for me, and I'm afraid that after a while, I depended on him too much."

Miguel remained silent, so Rosa continued. "Time went on, and the investigation grew cold. At the same time, Winston grew more and more obsessed with me. I felt cornered by him and trapped by my circumstances. Marrying him seemed inevitable." She gave Miguel a remorseful look. "I honestly don't know why it took so long for me to see I was in trouble and that I had a way out."

"But you did. That takes guts."

"I have to credit both my parents for helping me. It was an earnest plea from my father, just before he walked me down the aisle, that saved me."

"Way to go, Basil."

"You would do best to call him Mr. Reed."

"Ah, right."

CHAPTER 3

*R*osa enjoyed watching Miguel's reactions as they rode in the taxi from Heathrow Airport on an unusually bright and warm day. Of course, her parents had offered to pick them up, but Rosa wanted Miguel all to herself as he experienced being in London for the first time.

"Everyone talks like you," was his first remark at the airport terminal.

"Really? I've never noticed," Rosa teased.

"Do all the taxis look like this?" he asked once they got in the cab. "Black, I mean."

"Mostly, yes. We also call them hackney carriages."

Miguel pointed to the right-side steering wheel. "I'd be afraid to drive here."

"You'd get used to it, just as I had to in America."

Despite the eight-hour time difference and lack of sleep, Miguel seemed somehow energized. Everything was a curiosity, from the shiny black taxi driving on the left side of the road of narrow streets, to the iconic landmarks of St. Pauls Cathedral and Buckingham Palace.

As they drove through the district of Hammersmith, Miguel pointed. "That must've been the Thames back there on the right!" he jabbered. "Very famous river, you know."

Rosa laughed.

By the time they entered the Kensington district, he had grown quieter, though he still looked out the window in wonderment, commenting every so often on the narrow streets or the age of the buildings. This old world was a long way from youthful California.

Rosa found she had mixed feelings about being in London again. She still loved the city, but recent memories cast a pall over everything, despite the day being uncharacteristically sunny.

When the taxi finally pulled up to the front entrance of Hartigan House in South Kensington, Miguel was silent. Rosa guessed nervousness had taken over. She patted his hand and smiled reassuringly as they pulled to a stop.

"You'll do fine."

Miguel stared at the imposing house "Nice place you got here."

Rosa was struck by the differences between Hartigan House and the Forrester mansion. The sprawling Spanish-inspired Forrester mansion was only about twenty-five years old and constructed of wood with a plaster exterior. Hartigan House, a limestone three-story, had been built in the Victorian era, although it had obviously been well kept and modernized.

"Rosa! You made it!"

Rosa's parents had an indelible sophistication about them that hadn't faded with time. Ginger's red hair was streaked with gray and fashionably cut and styled with large curls falling at the nape of her neck. The wrinkles around her eyes had deepened, but the green-colored irises Rosa shared were as bright and vibrant as ever. As always, her mother dressed impeccably, her sense of style and her charming personality made her look ten or more years younger than her actual age.

Basil, entirely gray, had retained his full head of hair to the envy of many of his contemporaries. A pair of spectacles remained in place in front of his hazel eyes. His affair with cricket and tennis had kept him lean, even if his shoulders stooped forward a little. He was fashionably dressed in pleated trousers with well-pressed seams down the front and that narrowed at the ankles and fell on top of patent-leather loafers. His crisp white shirt and thin tie poked out from under a tartan waistcoat that presented him as distinctly British.

Ginger gave Rosa a big, American-style hug and a kiss on the cheek. Basil, though more reserved, followed suit. Obvious delight showed on both their faces at this joyful reunion. Rosa thought they had never looked so radiant.

"You look tired." Ginger stepped back at arm's length, appraising her daughter from top to bottom.

Basil remarked, "You look marvelous." His eyes were glistening.

"I'm not sure how I can be both," Rosa said with a laugh. "Unless I'm marvelously tired-looking."

"Such cheek," Ginger said with a tease.

Rosa motioned to Miguel, who was waiting beside their pile of luggage. "Mum, Dad, this is Detective Miguel Belmonte. Miguel, these are my parents, Mr. and Mrs. Reed."

"Pleased to meet you, young man." Basil shook

Miguel's hand, looking him straight in the eye. Rosa guessed that his grip had not weakened over the years.

"And you too, sir," Miguel said.

Ginger stepped forward and took Miguel's hand in both of hers and smiled warmly. "Welcome to Hartigan House. I hope you'll feel at home here."

"Thank you."

Rosa nudged him, and he quickly corrected, "Madam."

If there was any uncomfortableness with Miguel's ethnicity, Rosa couldn't detect it. Her parents were far too discreet for that. She had quietly wondered at what they would think at first, yet also had confidence any reservations would be overcome once they got to know Miguel. Both her parents were excellent judges of human character, so she had reason to assume they would not let a thing like race cloud their perceptions, even if it involved their only daughter.

In for a penny, in for a pound.

Just then, a tall, slim middle-aged man in a butler's uniform appeared at the door. He had prudently waited until the reunion was finished before appearing.

"Collins," Basil started, "please see to the luggage."

As they all turned to enter the house, Basil asked, "How do you like England so far, Detective Belmonte . . . or have you been here before?"

"No, sir, it's my first time. So far, I find it fascinating."

"You're lucky you came on a beautiful day," remarked Ginger. "It seems you brought the Californian sunshine with you."

Their footsteps and voices reverberated in the large entrance hall of Hartigan House, which featured black-and-white tiled floors and a large crystal chandelier hanging overhead from a vaulted ceiling.

"You must be tired, Detective Belmonte," Ginger said. "I'll show you to the guest room, and then we'll meet for some lunch if you're up for it."

Rosa saw Miguel look at his watch with surprise.

"Yes, it's only lunchtime," she offered. "I know it feels like it should be much later. But traveling through different time zones does tend to mix one up a bit."

Ginger led them up a wide staircase that circled up to the second floor in a crescent shape, giving the entrance its grand ceiling. When they reached the top landing, Ginger turned to Rosa. "You, of course, know where your room is." She nodded to the right. "Detective Belmonte, the guest room is down this way."

As they parted ways, Miguel shot Rosa a look, and she gave him a small wave of encouragement. The guest room was next to the library and very pleasant. It even had its own bathroom, a relatively new renovation.

Rosa stepped inside her bedroom and stood still. Was she *really* back here? It seemed surreal she'd been away for almost a year. This had been her room since she was a girl, and it had the same furnishings from when she was a young teenager, before her time in America. There was a large bed with an extravagantly carved wooden head and footboard. A full-length mirror and matching dressing table stood in the corner, with a chair sitting in front of two large windows that let in the natural light.

How often had she sat there brushing her hair in the morning while looking out at the lush gardens behind Hartigan House? She walked over to the window and looked out at the familiar view. An oak tree graced the corner of the garden.

As a young girl, Rosa had spent hours swinging back and forth on a wood-seated rope-swing that her father had hung for her from one of the larger, lower branches. She had dubbed it her 'thinking spot.' The swing was gone now, but Rosa smiled at the memory. It was beautiful, but she already missed the ocean.

The thought surprised her.

CHAPTER 4

*R*osa was proud of the way Miguel handled himself over lunch in the dining room at Hartigan House. Coming from a large family, his own experiences around a family meal were vastly different from her own. Although her parents were both easy conversationalists, Rosa recognized a familiar British formalness that would starkly contrast with the boisterous mealtimes she assumed were Miguel's experience being raised in a Mexican home.

At one point, Ginger excused herself and got up to consult with the cook in the kitchen while Basil turned to say something to the maid.

Rosa leaned in and whispered to Miguel. "You're doing great!"

Miguel slowly blew air out through pursed lips.

Basil turned back to Miguel. "You're quite young to be a detective. That's rather impressive."

"Thank you, Mr. Reed. I started my training as soon as the war ended. But as fast as I went through training, it seems Rosa beat me to it."

"Unfair head start, I would say," Ginger said as she returned to the table.

"You're the one with an impressive career, sir," Miguel said. "Twenty years a chief inspector and ten as a superintendent is no small thing."

"Indeed, I'm proud of my time at Scotland Yard." Basil cut into a piece of roast beef. "Although, all of that is rapidly fading in the rear view now."

"What about you, ma'am?" Miguel said to Ginger.

"We say, *madam*," Rosa corrected gently. "Ma'am is for the Queen."

Ginger chuckled. "He can call me ma'am if he likes."

"Forgive me," Miguel said. "What I mean to say is that Rosa has told me all about your career as a private investigator. I must say, I'm a bit intimidated."

Ginger waved her fingers. "Oh, pishposh. I fumbled my way through things like anyone would."

"Doesn't sound like fumbling to me. You had

your own office; what is it called again?" He turned to Rosa for help.

"Lady Gold Investigations."

"Right, that's it. Lady Gold Investigations. Rosa told me that's where she first was inspired to pursue the investigative business." Miguel recounted what Rosa had told him more than once. "Do you still keep that office?"

"Oh no," Ginger said. "I shut it down years ago. My primary concern has more to do with my dress shop, which is still going."

"The shop is called Feathers & Flair," Rosa said. "Mum is equally well known for being a follower of fashion as she is for her detective work."

"Hats and dresses," Basil offered. "Apparently, there's a real need for them in London." He grinned at Miguel. "I'm sure you find it as fascinating as I do." His mouth carried just the hint of a smirk.

"The shop is relaxing to run and rewarding in its own way," Ginger said. "There's a certain satisfaction in seeing a lady walking down the street dressed in a Pierre Balmain-inspired creation or a Balenciaga knowing she bought it at my shop."

"I'm sure Miguel is *very* familiar with those names," Basil quipped, not looking up from his meal.

"I mean, I still have an interest in detective work,"

Ginger said, ignoring the slight jibe. "I don't have the energy or time to take on clients anymore. Besides, I am not sure how appropriate it is for a lady at my stage of life to be dashing about chasing unsavory characters all over London."

"Be that as it may, if half of what Rosa told me is true, and I'm sure all of it is," Miguel said, "you have had a brilliant investigative career. I almost wish I could bring you both to Santa Bonita to act as consultants along with Rosa."

"Now *that* I would love to do," Ginger remarked. "I wouldn't mind a visit with Louisa. We could fly this time! What do you say, Basil?"

"That would depend entirely on the state of the cricket there. You can't expect me to go overseas for any length of time if there aren't any worthwhile cricket matches to attend." He smiled at Miguel. "Do you have cricket in Santa Bonita? It's the only *true* gentleman's sport, you know. Or perhaps civilization in the colonies has not yet reached that point."

"I . . . um . . ." Miguel stammered.

Rosa nudged his shoulder with hers. "He's only joking."

Rosa saw Miguel shoot a nervous glance at Basil, who gave him a wink while patting his lips with a napkin. "Perhaps we *should* go," Basil added. "There could be a desperate lack of hats there too!"

"Basil!" Ginger scolded. "The young man is tired and still on California time. If you're going to be prankish, at least wait until he has a night's rest." She looked at Miguel apologetically.

"Actually, I would love to see a cricket game," Miguel said.

"Jolly good, now that's the spirit!" Basil leaned back in his chair. "By the way, it's called a match not a game. Middlesex have just started their latest match at Lord's today, and it'll go on for another three days. When you're all rested and have a few hours to spare, I shall be glad to take you."

"You're a brave one," Ginger said, looking at Miguel with eyebrows raised as she lifted her fork to her mouth.

The conversation settled into the regular rhythm Rosa was used to when at home—her parents asking about the details of her life in Santa Bonita and inquiring as to Miguel's family and background. As Rosa had guessed, there was not a hint of the racial disdain or condescension that too often marked conversations at the Forresters. Instead, there was an honest curiosity mixed with the easy, witty banter she had been raised in and with which Miguel was also comfortable.

Rosa so enjoyed watching Miguel and her parents' pleasant engagement, she was almost reluctant to bring up the subject of the investigation.

"What have the police told you about the case?" Rosa asked. "What's the new lead?"

"It seems the police have had their sights on a known thief, a certain William Briggs, who has a record of violent behavior," Ginger said. "Apparently, he was known to be in the area at the time. Briggs is wanted in several counties for robbery including Cumbria and Yorkshire, as well as the city of Manchester."

"Lancashire too, love," Basil said.

"Oh yes, Lancashire as well, thank you, Basil. Chief Inspector Fredericks tells us he has a reputation for targeting affluent neighborhoods and had decided he wanted to try his luck in London."

"He's also known to be violent," Basil said. "In Carlisle, he broke into a large property, and when caught in the act by the butler, he attacked the poor fellow and left him for dead. The chap survived, though, and gave the police a vivid description. It matched perfectly with a description police already had from a witness in Manchester who saw a man climbing out of the second-story window of another residence in the middle of the night."

"How do the police know his name?" Miguel asked. "Has he been arrested before?"

"Yes," Basil said. "He served two years in prison in Manchester for armed robbery and assaulting a police officer. He was supposed to serve ten years but escaped, along with another inmate. That was eight years ago. The prison authorities are still trying to figure out exactly how they accomplished it. Police spotted Briggs in Sunderland in the summer of fifty-one, but he eluded them. Evidently, it was quite a footrace through the city. Local papers carried the story, much to the embarrassment of the police. It was a bit of a scandal that the local constables were outrun in a footrace."

"Just last week, Briggs was finally apprehended here in London," Ginger added.

"I guess a thief like that does best when changing locations from time to time," Miguel offered. "It makes it harder for the police to track him."

"It's a wonder he hasn't been caught more often," Basil said. "He must be quite cunning, eluding capture for most of his life and then escaping the prison."

Rosa thought for a moment and then looked at

her parents. "It sounds like he could be the killer, but is there any evidence that is more direct linking him to the murder?"

Basil answered, "When the police searched his things, they found a gold cufflink with W. Eveleigh inscribed on it."

"That's incriminating, all right." Rosa raised a brow. "What was his explanation for having it?"

"He claims to have won it in a poker game a few months earlier," Ginger said.

Miguel lifted his chin. "That would mean other players were there. Can his story be verified?"

"Briggs has provided three names," Ginger said, "but the men are also known criminals, and as such, not credible witnesses. Nor have they been easy to track down."

"The police are going to question Winston about that cufflink as soon as possible," Basil said. "I guess he didn't realize it's been missing and can't recall when or where he last saw it. I've lost a few of my own and can't answer for them. At any rate, Scotland Yard is investigating everything in earnest."

Ginger nodded. "Briggs admitted to being in the London area in March 1951 and confessed to robbing homes, but he swears he never went near Kenway House. His alibi is dodgy, to say the least. He insists he was in the company of a Mr. Jack Corning, another known burglar wanted by the police. Briggs claims he and Corning were together that night robbing a house in Chelsea."

"And was another home robbed that night?" Miguel asked.

"Yes, there was—the home of a wealthy and influential banker. But Corning is still at large, so the police have not been able to verify his involvement. No fingerprints."

"I imagine the robbery in Chelsea was in the papers," Rosa said.

Basil nodded. "Yes, so it's possible that Briggs could have read about it and remembered the case when the police questioned him. Also, a high-profile robbery occurring on the same night he murdered Vivien could have easily caught his attention. So, it's not out of the question."

Rosa's heart skipped a beat. Was this it? Had they found their man? "Do you think this Briggs is the killer?" she asked.

"The police are quite confident they have their man." Basil cleared his throat. "But they admit they need more time to bring the case to court. They are, of course, searching for Corning, but in the meantime, Briggs is being held for his other various crimes."

Rosa glanced at Miguel. It sounded promising. Perhaps the case *was* close to being solved. She had no way of tracking down Jack Corning, so she had to trust the police to do that.

Regardless, Rosa wouldn't rest until the killer was convicted and sentenced.

CHAPTER 5

*R*osa slept for fourteen hours straight and woke up feeling refreshed but hungry. She wondered how Miguel had fared during the night. She knew from experience that the first few nights after crossing eight time zones could be problematic for getting an entire night's rest, especially in a strange bed. After a good long soak in the tub, she dressed in blue trousers and a striped blouse with three-quarter length sleeves. She then made her way down to the morning room and found Miguel and her parents already there enjoying a breakfast of toast, sausages and eggs, along with fried tomatoes and mushrooms.

Basil looked up from his meal and smiled. "Ah, there's my girl."

"Good morning," Rosa said.

"Did you sleep well?" Ginger asked.

"I did, thank you." Rosa claimed a chair beside Miguel, who looked rested and happy. He smiled at her, refraining from the kiss she knew they both wanted, settling for her hand, which he squeezed under the table. "How did you do, Miguel?"

"As soon as my head hit the pillow, I was out. I haven't slept that deeply in years."

Rosa helped herself to the pot of tea sitting on the table, adding a little sugar before sipping. She then left Miguel's side to fill her plate with the breakfast fare waiting on the sideboard.

"Miguel and I were just discussing the day's schedule," Basil said. "Would you mind terribly if I stole your young man for a few hours this morning? Middlesex are playing Nottinghamshire, and I thought it would be great fun for him to join me for the last hour or two before lunch. Denis Compton is playing so it promises to be quite ripping."

Rosa arched a brow in Miguel's direction. "Are you sure you're up to that?" She added a smile, but her concern was sincere. "Spending the morning with Basil Reed at a cricket match is not for the faint of heart, you know."

"Oh, poppycock," Basil said before Miguel could

answer. "It's nothing this lad can't handle. I'll have him back by this afternoon in one piece. We'll take the underground and Bob's your uncle."

Miguel grinned at Rosa, delighting her with his dimples. "I *am* in London, and I want the full experience."

Ginger reached across the table and patted Rosa's forearm. "We can entertain ourselves while they're away, love."

"Feathers & Flair?" Rosa asked. She'd promised Gloria she'd bring her a new dress, something European.

"Oh, yes," Ginger said. "But I also thought we might visit Mr. Briggs."

Miguel dropped his fork.

Basil slowly turned his head. "Ginger?"

"I've already rung the prison to arrange it. Governor Willis owes me a favor, you see. We'll be behind a screen. It's hardly dangerous. We'll report back to both of you after lunch."

Rosa bit her lips to keep from smiling. The years hadn't dimmed her mother's resolve and determination. Ginger Reed, also known as Lady Gold, was an enigma to most. A charming, fashionable socialite on the outside and a clever and perspicacious soul on the inside.

Basil lifted his palms in surrender then gave Miguel a sideways glance. "There's no use in arguing with a Reed lady. Even when you think you've got your way, you realize later you were beguiled into theirs."

Miguel laughed. "Believe me, sir. I've already discovered that is true." He turned to Rosa. "And what about your uncle Bob? Will he be joining us later?"

Basil and Rosa shared a look and then burst out laughing.

A short while later, Ginger and Rosa headed through the back entrance of the house and the garden to the garage. Built of limestone, the garage had been kept up-to-date with fresh paint on its wooden doors, opened earlier by one of the staff. Inside was a sparkling green two-door sports car.

Rosa gasped. "It's beautiful!"

"It's called an MG Roadster. It has a rather powerful engine. Sixty-eight horsepower!"

Rosa's hand went to her lips to hide the fact that her mouth had dropped open. "I absolutely adore it!" She placed her hand on the long-nose hood, admiring the chrome grille, round headlamps, and chrome wire-spoked wheels.

"Well, if you behave yourself," Ginger said as she

smiled and jingled her keys in the air, "I might let you drive back home later."

Ginger turned the key, and the engine rumbled to life. She slowly backed the car out of the garage, into the back alley, and onto the street. Then she accelerated quickly, the car's engine responding immediately. Rosa couldn't help a giggle as the tires chirped slightly as they rounded the first corner.

It was always a thrill driving with her mother.

As they headed north toward Watford, Rosa took in all the familiar sights. So many memories—good and bad—seemed to flood back at once. She'd had a happy childhood until the war years, but since then, her emotional attachments to the city had become entangled with feelings of heartache. Love lost when she left Miguel in California, friendship lost when Vivien was killed, and just an overall loss of innocence as London, which had been reduced to rubble, was slowly rebuilt.

"Scout sends his greetings," Ginger said. "He's so sorry it didn't work out for him to come to London. He's purchasing horses in Istanbul."

"I'm sad to miss seeing him," Rosa said.

Her brother, a former jockey and now a racehorse trainer, was twelve years her senior. He had left the house for boarding school before she was talking. During her adolescence, he had been too busy having his own adventures as a young man to spend much time at Hartigan House. An unfortunate horse-riding injury had kept him from the battlefield for most of the war, but he did his bit for the army by training horses for inhospitable terrain.

"To be fair," Rosa continued, "I hardly gave any notice about my return."

"Which is why you've missed out on seeing Aunt Felicia and Uncle Charles. Your cousins are with them too."

"Aren't they still living in France?" The Continent wasn't so far away that her relatives couldn't journey over.

"Yes," Ginger said, "but they've gone away for a few months. They bought a villa in Greece."

"I suppose meeting you and Dad is enough for Miguel to digest at the moment."

Ginger chuckled. "I like Miguel. He seems a decent sort, and I'm happy we are finally able to meet him."

After the war, Rosa had come back from her time with the Forresters so heartsick and melancholy that she confessed to her parents what had transpired with Miguel. They had judged him fairly back then:

Miguel had proposed, after all, and it was Rosa who had resisted at the time.

But, as the years went on, Miguel was all but forgotten, at least by her parents, and eventually, Winston entered the picture.

Winston Eveleigh and Miguel Belmonte couldn't be any more different. Miguel came from humbler circumstances but was a better man. Thankfully, Basil and Ginger Reed were astute enough to see that.

"I'm happy too. I can't believe that I'm getting a second chance with him."

Rosa caught Ginger's glance directed her way.

"You're in love with him?"

"Yes, Mum. I have been ever since I was seventeen."

CHAPTER 6

*S*tanfield Prison, in Watford, was one of England's newest prisons, and Rosa thought it wasn't as imposing as some of the older facilities in London such as Brixton or Wormwood Scrubs. Although the entire compound was made of the familiar redbrick construction, and like any other prison, there was barbed wire and guard towers, there had at least been an effort to use bright colors on the wood trim and doors.

After a quick security check, Rosa and Ginger were met by a tall white-haired man in his late fifties wearing a brown suit jacket over a white, collared shirt and black tie. He introduced himself as Mr. Thomson.

"I'll 'ave a guard posted in the room with ya.

Briggs is quite 'appy to receive visitors and 'e's never been one to 'old back in a conversation, if you get my meanin'." Mr. Thomson led them down several hallways, up a flight of stairs, and through several security doors.

The last door opened to a room intended for visitors. A heavy steel table was divided by a screen. On one side of it were two empty wooden chairs, which Mr. Thomson indicated were for Rosa and Ginger.

Briggs, a man of about forty and dressed in a prisoner's uniform, waited on the other side, chained to a steel ring bolted to the table. He smiled mirthlessly when he saw them, staring with steel-blue eyes. His dry lips parted, revealing crooked, tobacco-stained teeth.

A burly middle-aged guard, who'd been standing outside the door, followed them inside. "Take as much time as needed," Mr. Thomson said. He motioned to the guard. "Officer Grimes will be at your service if you need anythin'." He nodded at the guard then left the room.

"Welcome, ladies," William Briggs said in a dry voice. "I'd stand up an' give a proper greetin', but as you can see . . ." He lifted his manacled hand. "I don't think it's 'ardly fittin' for a peaceful man such as meself to 'ave this particular piece o' jewelry, but there you 'ave it."

Rosa glanced at Ginger, who nodded subtly. Though they hadn't made a clear pronouncement, Rosa's mother knew this case belonged to Rosa.

"My name is Miss Rosa Reed, and this is my mother, Mrs. Reed." Police training had taught her how to give unflinching eye contact. "Thank you for agreeing to speak to us."

"I'm pleased to make yo'r acquaintance. I don't 'ave many visitors. So, when they told me you two were comin', I put on me Sunday best." He chuckled at his own words and winked at Rosa. "I 'ad no idea you two would be so lovely lookin'." He smiled crookedly. "An' a mother and daughter to boot!"

Both Rosa and her mother took out notepads from their handbags, which did not escape William Briggs' notice.

"Blimey. You two are serious!"

"Were you 'working' in London in the autumn of fifty-one?"

He smirked. "Girl gets right to the point!"

Rosa kept his gaze.

"Okay, ah, yeah, I suppose so. That was six years ago. I 'ardly remember where I was any day beyond me time spent in this lovely establishment,"

Rosa doubted that. "A lady was murdered," she said sternly.

"Ah, You mean the Eveleigh woman, the rich one. I already told the coppers I 'ad nothin' to do with that. I'm a thief, I admit it. An' a darn good one until they trapped me."

"But you have a history of breaking into houses, taking things that don't belong to you, and on occasion, resorting to violence."

"I ain't never killed no one. Besides, I stay away from posh 'ouses. Too much trouble, they are. Guard dogs, alarms, connections with powerful people."

"Yet you claim to have been involved in a robbery in Chelsea that night," Rosa challenged.

"Yeah, with me ol' pal Jake," he said smugly. "I already told the police that."

"Unfortunately, Mr. Corning isn't around to be a witness for your alibi," Ginger said.

"No 'e's not, and ya can bet if I knew where 'e was 'olin' up right now, I'd certainly tell the coppers."

A worried expression passed quickly through the thief's eyes. "I'm not in the mood to 'ang for any murder, especially one I didn't commit. Jake, the snake, took all the money we stole from that banker. I 'aven't seen it, nor 'im ever since that night. No honor among thieves, they say." He sniffed derisively. "It was Jake that insisted we wear gloves that night so we wouldn't leave fingerprints. I told 'im I didn't need 'em but did it anyway. I should never 'ave gave in to 'im in the end. If they'd have found a nice ol' fingerprint of mine, the police wouldn't 'ave tried t' pin that lady's murder on me."

"What about the cufflink?" Rosa asked. "You must realize that your story about winning it in a poker game is pretty suspect. Where is the other one, Mr. Briggs?"

Mr. Briggs shook his head before answering. "I told the coppers a 'undred times already, I don't 'ave it, and I never did. The game took place in an 'otel room in South London just a few weeks ago. The bloke I won it from said 'e won it in another game the week before. I 'ave no idea what 'appened to the matching cufflink."

"Mr. Briggs," Rosa began, "if you didn't break into the Eveleigh residence in March nineteen fifty-one, do you know who did? I imagine there is talk among thieves."

Briggs sat back. "I'd love to 'elp. I really mean it. I am always tryin' to be a good citizen," He smiled at his own sarcasm, "But I 'ave no idea who done that deed. Now if you'll excuse me," He raised his free hand. "Guard. I'd like to go back to me penthouse suite."

Rosa's heart was heavy as she and her mother climbed back into the MG. Both just stared out of the front windshield in silence for a moment before Ginger started the car.

"Is he guilty, Mum?" Rosa asked. Had she actually looked Vivien's killer in the eye?

Rosa considered her mother, who didn't answer right away.

Finally, Ginger said, "It's hard to tell with people like that. He's lied his entire life and probably doesn't even know when he's doing it anymore."

"But do they have any actual proof he did it?" Rosa asked. "Or is it all circumstantial?"

"The police have witnesses who say that Mr. Briggs was in London in March, nineteen fifty-one," Ginger said. "There was also a string of other robberies during that time, and most recently, Mr. Briggs' fingerprints were matched to a few found at other crime scenes. Until now, the police didn't know whose fingerprints they were." Ginger took a breath and let it out slowly. "But even with the cufflink, there is, unfortunately, room for doubt. It could still go either way in court."

Ginger put the car into gear and pointed it

toward London. "For one thing, why would a man like Briggs hold on to a cufflink after all these years? I would think he would have sold it for cash years ago.

"Oh, Mum, I was so hopeful that it was all over," Rosa said. "I don't know what I'll do if a clever lawyer finds a way to get Briggs acquitted based on insufficient evidence."

Ginger reached over and patted Rosa's shoulder. "Perhaps you need to take a brief break from the case. Why don't you call up your old friends? Perhaps some of your colleagues from the Metropolitan Police? Take Miguel on a tour of the city. Make some fresh memories of London. I'll bet he would love an afternoon at Selfridges!"

Rosa tried to imagine Miguel enjoying a five-story department store.

Keeping her eyes on the road ahead, Ginger said, "I should've mentioned that Winston rang for you this morning."

Rosa shot her mother a look. It wasn't like her to withhold information like that, though, she was glad not to have known about it before now.

"What did he want?"

"To see you, naturally." Her green eyes, wrinkled

at the corners, flashed with mischief. "I told him you were busy entertaining an overseas guest."

Rosa chuckled. "I doubt he was happy to hear that."

"No. Indeed he wasn't. I was shocked to learn he'd gone to Santa Bonita. I can only assume he intended to pursue you again?"

"Yes. Even though I never gave him any reason to believe the outcome between us could change. I'd stopped answering his letters or phone calls. After what I did to him, I'm quite honestly flummoxed by his continued interest. I would've thought he would despise me over it."

Ginger offered a sympathetic smile. "Did he meet Miguel there?"

"Oh yes, and you can imagine how that went down. I'm so proud of Miguel's handling of the condescension that came off Winston in waves."

"I can only imagine."

Rosa wished the MG had those new seat belt contraptions. She held on for dear life as her mother picked up speed.

AT AN EARLY EVENING dinner in the dining room of Hartigan House, the four ate delicious stew and dumplings while Basil regaled them about cricket and Miguel's ongoing bafflement.

"I hope I don't sound like a braggart when I say I'm good at playing baseball," Miguel said, "but cricket is beyond me."

"Oh, you catch on over time," Rosa said. "I hear it helps if you wear white."

"Ah," Miguel said. "That would explain everything." He slapped his forehead with his palm. "I wore the wrong colors."

They shared a laugh, then Miguel, growing more somber, asked, "How did it go at the prison?"

Rosa and Ginger shared their experiences and insights.

"If only Mr. Briggs had left evidence at the scene," Basil said. "How I'd love to put this torrid affair to bed."

Ginger reached for his hand. "We all would, love. But, if Mr. Briggs is innocent in this case, it's not helpful to Vivien's memory to hang the wrong man."

"*If* he's innocent," Basil said. "I've had the misfortune of encountering Mr. Briggs before. He and his ilk are rarely innocent."

"If he's guilty, Dad," Rosa started, "then we must find conclusive proof of his guilt. Somehow, some way."

When dinner ended, they retired to the sitting room, leaving the cleaning up to the kitchen staff.

Basil poured brandy for everyone, but Miguel raised a palm, declining. "I'm afraid if I drink that, I'll nod off in my chair."

"Me too," Rosa said. The fatigue of travel and the time change were landing hard. "Actually, Mum, Dad, I hope you don't mind if we retire early. We can start again in the morning."

"Of course, dear," Ginger said.

Rosa and Miguel said goodnight, leaving Basil and Ginger sitting on a settee, each with a glass of brandy in their hands and a smile on their face. It was a familiar scene for Rosa, having often watched her parents relax together in the evening in this very manner.

Rosa took Miguel's hand. "I want to show you something."

As they headed up the staircase, Miguel teased. "Just how excited should I be?"

Rosa nudged him playfully. "It's about the case!"

After one flight up to the attic and a walk to the end of the corridor, she opened a closed door. "This used to be a storage room. In fact a lady was once murdered here, her bones discovered by my mother when she moved back to London from Boston."

Miguel scoffed. "You're kidding?"

"I'm not. The remains had been trapped here for ten years when Hartigan House was shut up. When Vivien died, I turned it into my case room. I vowed to leave it this way until her killer was caught."

The room was small with a simple desk, a single armchair with a red cushion, and a floor lamp. The wall acted like an investigative board filled with notes, photographs, and sketches which were pinned to it. Different colored strings connected the pinned items. A two-by-three-foot blackboard hung on the adjacent wall. The only things written on the blackboard were two large question marks.

Rosa watched Miguel's expression moving from astonishment to fascination. His eyes narrowed as he studied each item and grimaced when he came to the photographs of Vivien's body lying on the carpet. There were several close-up shots of bruises on her neck, though her dark hair covered most of her face. Other photographs included a large study, with Winston's desk, a mess of papers scattered along the top of it and on the floor. A chair was tipped over, and a lamp lay broken nearby. The bottom pane of the window was broken out, with a hole large enough for a man to crawl through.

"I would spend hours staring at that blasted wall,"

Rosa said. "I thought it might help me sort it all out." An unexpected rush of emotion welled up as she stood there, suddenly feeling fragile. Then, with a choked voice, she added, "It didn't."

Miguel pulled her into a warm embrace. "We are going to get this guy," he breathed. "If it's Briggs, we'll prove it. And if it's not, we'll find the culprit. I won't rest until we do."

CHAPTER 7

*H*aving slept in until almost noon, Rosa decided to take Miguel to one of her favorite haunts for dinner. The Whistling Dog was the unofficial social spot for many of the Metropolitan Police constables. Almost any day of the week, Rosa could hop on the underground and be at the restaurant within minutes. Once there, she would often find a few tables occupied by members of the Metropolitan Police Force, both men and women, the latter being a rarity. Rosa had shared many good laughs and interesting conversations sitting in that old meeting spot.

After a time, though, Winston had insisted that he accompany her every time she went and managed to put a damper on things, particularly as he tended to look down his nose at her colleagues. As a result, she'd stopped going almost a year before her sudden departure from London. In hindsight, Rosa wondered how she'd gotten to a point where she'd become so easily controlled.

She and Miguel crossed the narrow street toward the building. When they stepped inside, they were hit with loud chatter and the strong smell of tobacco smoke. The place had low, wood-beamed ceilings and a redbrick hearth, with a fire blazing that served to warm the room. The place was almost full, and no one paid them any notice as they stepped in.

"Wow. How old did you say this place was?" Miguel ducked under one of the beams, barely clearing his head.

"About three hundred years old, I think."

Miguel whistled. "Older than my gramma."

"There's a seating area down the stairs," Rosa said. She led Miguel through the crowded room to the back, where a winding brick stairway opened underground. The domed ceiling was painted white, making it less tomb-like. Only half-full, it was quieter than the room above.

"Was this the dungeon?" Miguel asked as they stood at the bottom of the stairwell, peering into the dimly lit chamber.

"It's a tavern!" Rosa laughed. "If you want to see a dungeon, we'll go to the Tower of London tomorrow."

A male voice boomed from the far side of the room. "WPC Reed!"

"Ah," Rosa said. "I knew we'd see someone." She grabbed Miguel's hand and approached a table filled with members of the Met.

"So good to see you, Constable Halstead," Rosa said.

Constable Cyril Halstead was a short but athletic-looking man with close-cropped hair and a friendly demeanor.

"Please, join us." He gestured to two empty chairs.

Rosa recognized most of the people at the table and greeted them warmly. All eyes were on her and Miguel as they took a seat, especially on Miguel.

As a runaway bride, Rosa's fame had preceded her, and an awkward silence fell before Constable Halstead broke it, speaking a tad louder than needed.

"For those of you who don't know, WPC Reed is the daughter of Superintendent Basil Reed, a former policewoman at the Met, and rumor has it—" He raised his glass and nodded to Miguel. "She's the current official goodwill ambassador to California."

Everyone chuckled. Rosa's face reddened slightly at the sudden attention.

"The rumors are true." She motioned to Miguel at her side. "This is Detective Miguel Belmonte from the Santa Bonita Police Force."

Several "aahs" and "oohs" could be heard from the table as Miguel smiled shyly and waved.

The conversations around the table soon resumed. Answering several questions about her new life in California, Rosa shared stories from her past few months there. At one point, Rosa divulged that she had met Elvis Presley less than six months earlier at a concert in Santa Bonita in connection with another murder case she had worked on. That became the focus of the discussion for quite a while. Apparently, Elvis's hit, "Heartbreak Hotel," was popular in London at the moment.

As the evening wore on and Rosa and Miguel ordered their food, the drinks kept flowing, and conversations soon grew increasingly boisterous. Pleased to see Miguel laughing and joking as if he'd been part of this gang for years, Rosa reached under the table to squeeze his hand. It felt good to share this moment of reconnection with him. His demeanor was so different from Winston's snobbery.

"Of course I remember Lady Vivien."

Rosa's ears immediately locked on to a conversation further down the table.

"She might have made an excellent solicitor, and it's sad what happened to her, but quite honestly, one could've expected it."

Rosa stared at the two women, a blonde and a brunette—wives or girlfriends of the constables they were with—engaged in a conversation, words slurring. Rosa vaguely recognized the blonde but couldn't quite place her.

"Shhh . . . ," the brunette warned, her eyes darting apologetically to Rosa.

"I know, I know. I'll shut up now."

Finally, it came to Rosa. The chatty blonde had been a friend of Vivien's, a fellow law student. Rosa had only met her once.

She leaned toward Cyril Halstead, speaking with her back turned to the opposite end of the table. "Who is the tall lady, sitting four chairs down on my right?"

"That's Joan Freeman. She was seeing a constable who was transferred to Liverpool, but she just kind of kept on hanging around with us after that ended. Her friend is Debbie Waldren."

"Well, she led them on then, didn't she?" Miss Freeman said.

Rosa and Miguel, along with the entire table, stared at Miss Freeman, whose voice had risen several levels louder. "I mean, who knows what jilted lover had followed her home? I don't want to say she got what she deserved, but you know . . . let's just say there's more to it than everybody thinks."

Rosa's anger flared.

Her mind flashed back to the investigation. The police had thoroughly checked with any boyfriends that Vivien might have had and found nothing out of the ordinary. Not one to lead men on, Vivien had dated only two men in her young life. Both had insisted that their relationship with Vivien had always been amicable and Rosa knew this to be true.

Suddenly, Miss Freeman pushed back her chair, stood as if in slow motion, and weaved to the women's restroom.

"I'll be right back," Rosa said to Miguel, then got up to follow.

Rosa quietly waited until Joan had finished in the toilet stall. But Joan didn't seem to notice her standing there as she staggered to the sink. Then, when she did finally notice, her face registered a dull, momentary surprise.

"Oh, hello, WPC Reed." She pulled out a tube of lipstick.

"Hi, Miss Freeman. It's Miss Reed now."

"Oh, yeah, just habit, eh?"

"Yes. Please forgive me, but I couldn't help hearing what you said about Lady Vivien."

Miss Freeman leaned closer to the mirror and applied lipstick but didn't respond.

"I'm just wondering what you meant by Lady Vivien leading men on."

Miss Freeman snorted as she struggled to put the cap back on the lipstick tube.

"I just mean, I never saw any evidence of that, and Lady Vivien and I were very close."

"Were you now?" Miss Freeman patted her short curls.

"You were living in London about the time of her death, were you not?" Rosa asked.

Miss Freeman turned to Rosa and leaned against the sink. "Should I be summoning a solicitor?"

Rosa noticed the glassy look in Miss Freeman's eyes and worried she might fall over.

"Of course not," Rosa said. "I only wonder if you have any idea who might have killed her."

Miss Freeman snorted derisively. "A burglar

caught in the act! The police said as much when they interviewed me."

"But you don't believe that. I heard you say so. You said there's more to it."

Miss Freeman shook her head and smirked. "Yes, well, perhaps some burglars are not *really* burglars. I . . ." She seemed to consider something for a moment. "I don't think I want to talk to you. I'm a little sozzled, and I'm going home now." She straightened up and wobbled past Rosa and out the door. Rosa followed her up the stairs.

Suddenly, Miss Freeman stopped on the steps and, hanging tightly to the rail, whirled around to face Rosa. "Don't you dare follow me!"

Miss Freeman's strong reaction bewildered Rosa, who had the feeling that the cold case of Vivien's murder might just have turned up a few degrees.

CHAPTER 8

s Rosa and Miguel made their way through the crowded upper level of the tavern toward the front entrance, a familiar voice called out.

"Rosa!"

At a corner table, sitting by himself and smoking a cigarette, was Lord Winston Eveleigh. He stood up and gestured for them to join him. Rosa glanced at Miguel, who nodded. Rosa took a breath then clutched his hand as they wove through the tables.

Winston wore his usual gray sports jacket and a white collared shirt with a blue ascot. Miguel and Rosa each claimed an empty chair. "I remembered this as one of your haunts, Rosa," he said. "I rang your parents, and they told me you were out. So, I took a chance you might come here tonight."

"We were just about to leave," Rosa said. "We've been here for a couple of hours already, catching up with a few of my former colleagues from the Met."

"Ah, good for you." Winston blew smoke into the air, the plume billowing to the ceiling, joining the cloud of smoke gathered there. "It's good to see old friends again, I suspect." He nodded curtly to Miguel. "Belmonte. I must say, I'm surprised you came all this way."

"I wanted to help with the investigation," Miguel said.

"Really?" Winston's eyebrows went up as he looked at Rosa. "You mean to tell me you intend to pursue the case after all?"

After Winston had expressly told her not to? "Yes," Rosa said simply.

A look of disappointment crossed Winston's face as he exhaled cigarette smoke and then put out the cigarette in the ceramic ashtray. "I spoke to Chief Inspector Fredericks this morning," he said. "He told me that although they still have only circumstantial evidence, they are confident they have their man. There is probably not much left to investigate. I'm sure you've heard that he had one of my cufflinks."

"Yes. By the way, why didn't you mention that you were missing a cufflink in the initial investigation?"

"I didn't realize it was gone. Those cufflinks weren't my favorite, and I rarely wore them."

"Even if I can't help with the investigation, I'm glad Miguel could meet my parents and see where I grew up," Rosa said.

As if Miguel weren't sitting right there, Winston looked directly at Rosa. "He must've been a bit of a surprise for your parents." One corner of his mouth pulled up in a half-smirk—a trademark look for Lord Winston Eveleigh that Rosa knew too well.

Winston finally cast another glance at Miguel. "How do you like London so far, Belmonte?"

"I think it's fascinating," Miguel said. "So much interesting history and culture to be found here."

"Yes," Winston murmured. "Unlike where you grew up, I'm sure."

"History and culture are to be found in America too," Rosa said, feeling defensive of her new home state. "I find it just as fascinating in California as Miguel does here. I'm thrilled to have been allowed to see beyond the boundaries of England. Not only that, Europe has nothing to the unspoiled grandeur of nature in America."

Rosa wasn't quite sure where that little speech came from.

"I'm enjoying getting to know Rosa's parents," Miguel said after an awkward moment of silence.

"Dad took him to see a cricket match at Lord's yesterday," Rosa said brightly. It brought her a slight sense of satisfaction to see a look of consternation flash across Winston's face. Basil had never expressed an interest in doing anything with Winston, much less attend a cricket match.

"Middlesex versus Nottinghamshire," Miguel added. "It was um . . . *ripping.*" He borrowed Basil's own words, which made Rosa smile.

Winston focused his attention back on Rosa. "How are they, by the way? I mean to call into Hartigan House soon."

"They're doing very well," Rosa said. "I'll be sure to let them know you asked about them."

As she pushed away from the table, Rosa suddenly had another thought.

"Winston, I meant to ask you, what have you done with all of Vivien's things?"

"Oh, they're still in boxes at home, stored in one of her wardrobes. I have been meaning to distribute them to charity for years now, but it's just one of those things I keep forgetting."

"I had started sorting and packing those things years ago," Rosa said, "but I never had the emotional fortitude to finish the job. I would like to call in this week sometime and have another crack at it."

"Of course. I'll be out almost every day this week, but I'll alert the staff that you will be coming."

"Thank you," Rosa said, feeling sincere gratitude. "Well, we should get going." She glanced at Miguel, who nodded.

"Will you be staying here in London much longer?" Winston asked. He looked at Miguel. "I assume you haven't left your job in Santa Bonita."

"No, I haven't. But I had vacation time coming, and I think things are being looked after well enough until I get back."

Winston's eyebrows went up in a gesture of resignation. He sighed and pulled out another cigarette.

"We're not sure yet how long we'll stay," Rosa said. "I haven't quite finished . . . you know, looking into things regarding the case."

Winston shook his head. "It's all but grown cold again."

"Perhaps," Rosa admitted then recalled her strange encounter with the woman in the restroom. "Do you happen to know a Miss Joan Freeman?"

Winston's pupils dilated, followed by a slight twitch in his cheek. Clearly, the question had caught him off guard.

"Now that's a name I would rather forget," he finally said. "Where on earth did you hear it?"

"Downstairs," Miguel answered. "Tonight. She was here with Rosa's friends."

"She left about an hour ago," Rosa added. "She knew Vivien."

"Good God." Winston snorted. "I'm glad I missed her."

"So, you do know her?" Rosa pressed.

"Yes, yes. I know her, or rather *knew* her. If I'd any idea she might be hanging about here tonight, I wouldn't have come."

Rosa's curiosity was piqued. "Why not?"

"Really, Rosa. Must I get into the gruesome details? Why are you asking?"

"I overheard her speaking poorly of Vivien tonight. When I asked her about it, she grew angry and left."

Winston stared at Rosa, his eyes flickering with indecision. Then he said, "She and I were . . . involved for a brief time. A long time ago. Before you and I were engaged. She didn't take it well when I broke it off and hounded me for weeks after. I finally confronted her, and matters got frightfully distasteful. She even attacked me with a paring knife. Fortunately, I can handle myself quite well." He adjusted his ascot while glancing at Miguel. "Anyway, that's the end of the story. From what I heard, she was into another poor bloke. I heard it was one of your constable colleagues."

"Why on earth have you never mentioned this to the police or me?" Rosa asked, feeling incredulous. And suspicious. Winston said he and Miss Freeman had been together before Rosa and Winston were engaged. What about the months of dating before then? Had he not been true to her?

"Why would I?" Winston returned.

"*Motive*, Winston," Rosa said. "Miss Freeman resented you breaking up with her. She might've wanted to get back at you by robbing you, or worse, killing your only sibling."

"Many murders have been committed out of revenge by a former lover," Miguel added. "It's surprising how unhinged people can become."

Winston smirked as he slowly shook his head. "For a couple of detectives, you're both far off the mark. A burglar followed my movements for a few days, then broke into Kenway House while I was out. Vivien caught him in the act, and it ended violently.

I'll wager you've seen plenty of cases like that as well, Belmonte."

Winston locked his gaze on Rosa. "I loved my sister and was devastated when she died. You know that, Rosa. It took me a long time to forgive myself for not going home that night. Thankfully, I have been able to move on." He leaned back and sighed. "You, on the other hand, don't seem to have that capacity. Joan Freeman? Don't be ridiculous. She's an obnoxious woman, a momentary anomaly, but I can't believe she'd kill my sister over a lovers' tiff."

CHAPTER 9

The next afternoon Miguel and Rosa sat in the Macabre Coffee Shop in Soho, sipping on dark coffee. The Italian-made espresso machine loudly announced another cup ready for an eager customer. Rosa thought it a bit of a nuisance, not so much because it interrupted conversations in the crowded cafe, but because it also interfered with the musical combo in the corner. Three young men played guitars and sang, but hardly anyone was listening. That was, of course, except Miguel.

"They're very good," he said while his head bobbed to the beat.

Rosa agreed. "What style of music would you call that?"

"I think they call it *skiffle*."

"I like your band better." Rosa poised an elbow on the table, rested her fist under her chin, and batted her eyelashes. Then, with a teasing lilt, she added, "Mick and the Beat Boys are just the coolest, and the lead singer, Miguel, is a real dreamboat."

Miguel laughed. "Golly gee. So kind of you to say. Though I don't have any illusions that we'll be big stars someday. But these guys, I don't know. They have something . . ." His voice trailed off as he listened.

"Thanks a million, ladies and gentlemen," the boyish-looking lead singer said in a thick Liverpool accent. "We'll be back after a short break."

"I don't know what he's thanking them for; no one's even listening," Rosa said.

As they were putting down their instruments, Miguel waved the young man over.

"You guys are terrific," he said.

The lad stuffed his fists into his jacket pockets. "Thanks. This is our first adventure outside Liverpool. I'm John." He reached out his hand to Miguel and nodded to Rosa. "John Lennon. We call ourselves The Quarrymen."

"It's a good combo," Miguel offered. "I have a band myself, and I think you guys are way out. I'll remember your name for when I see you on *The Ed Sullivan Show* one day."

John chuckled. "Imagine us playing in America! But I appreciate the compliment." John thanked Miguel again and turned to join his bandmates, who were already eating.

Just then, Debbie Waldren, the brunette friend of Joan Freeman, entered the café. She waved when she saw Miguel and Rosa.

"I'm sorry for being late," she said, putting her handbag on the table and settling into the empty chair.

When Rosa and Miguel had left Winston the night before, they'd ended up on the pavement as Miss Waldren exited the tavern. To Rosa's surprise and pleasure, Miss Waldren had agreed to meet up.

"I've to go to work in an hour. I'm a receptionist at The Burlington, a hotel not far from here." She took a deep breath and then smiled at them both. "Did you two plan to do any sightseeing today?"

"Miguel wants to get his picture taken with Winston Churchill at Madame Tussauds."

Miguel grinned. "And see the Tower of London."

"As every visitor to London must," Miss Waldren said with a chuckle. She ordered a coffee from the waitress and removed her short button-down jacket, hanging it on the back of the chair.

"Thanks for agreeing to meet us," Rosa said.

"It's no problem. I'm not sure how I can help. As I told you last night, Joan and I aren't that close, despite what it might have looked like. Joan had a wee bit too much to drink. A bad habit these days."

"How long have you known her?" Miguel asked.

"Oh, about ten years. She studied law at one time, but she gave that up and works as the manager of housekeeping at the hotel where I work." She glanced away. "Our friendship took a bit of a turn some time ago, and I had to distance myself from her a bit. Last night was what you'd call an accidental meeting."

"What happened?" Rosa asked.

"You know, it was a few months before Lady Vivien died. Joan's a bit of an obsessive person and can be frightfully vindictive sometimes. And at times, that spite turned on me. Anyway, I know you heard her saying things last night. I think she knew you and Lady Vivien were close, and she got going on that subject again last night when she saw you."

"Do you know why she said the things she did?" Rosa asked.

"Well, I do have a suspicion." A waitress brought

a coffee, and Debbie stirred in cream and sugar as she spoke. "I didn't know Lady Vivien Eveleigh nor Lord Winston Eveleigh, but I do know that Joan was not fond of Lady Vivien."

"You mean, because of her wealth?"

"No, nothing like that. I remember she'd gossip about Lady Vivien from time to time; this was before Lady Vivien's death. I finally told her to stop. I don't like that sort of thing. Anyway, she told me then that a friend of hers, Clive Blackmore, was interested in Lady Vivien, or at least Joan thought so, but apparently, Lady Vivien didn't want anything to do with him. I think she might have just started seeing another man."

"I got the distinct feeling that Joan was soft on this Clive fellow and resented that he didn't feel the same way. That's why she talked last night about Lady Vivien leading men on."

"Did you ever talk about this with the police?" Miguel asked.

"No. It never came up. I mean, they were trying to find someone who had something against Lord Winston Eveleigh. No one ever asked me about Lady Vivien. Why would they? I didn't even know her."

. . .

A HALF-HOUR LATER, Rosa and Miguel hopped aboard the underground train at Tottenham Court Road tube station to head back to High Street Kensington station.

"I don't know if I would ever get used to this," Miguel said as the train pulled away from the platform. "All these underground passages are bewildering. Then you step on one of these little trains and go through dark tunnels at God knows how fast, and suddenly, you see light and *bingo*; you've just traveled to a whole different neighborhood. It's eerie."

"You've never used the Los Angeles subway system?"

"I never got a chance. It was shut down almost two years ago. Besides, I don't think it was anything like this."

"Londoners rely heavily on the underground, of course. It's quite convenient. A lot of the time, it's faster than going by car. We'll use it tomorrow to go and do some more sightseeing. Perhaps I'll take you to Piccadilly Circus."

Miguel looked surprised. "There's a circus in London?"

"It's not an actual circus," Rosa explained. "It's an area where there's lots of shopping, restaurants and things like that. The word 'circus' is from Latin. It means 'circle.' The Romans must have named it."

Miguel grinned, his dimples making an appearance. "The Romans, huh?"

"I'm joking." Rosa flicked a palm. "Besides, you missed the point. I said 'shopping.'"

"Of course. That sounds wonderful!"

"I sense sarcasm."

Miguel smirked. "Not at all."

"Well, if you like shopping so much, I can take you to Selfridges. That's a huge department store on Oxford Street."

"Jolly good. But of course, I should like to visit the Queen after that," Miguel said, amusing Rosa with his attempt at a posh accent.

"We could call in at Buckingham Palace," she said, "but a personal visit might be hard to arrange. From what I've read, there's a bit of a scandal going on right now."

"Oh, oh. Trouble at Buckingham? Did one of those royal guards finally break into a smile?"

"Nothing *that* serious!" Rosa mocked a look of horror. "No, the Duke of Edinburgh's best friend and personal secretary, Lieutenant Commander Michael Parker, is getting divorced. Something to do with a scandalous party that took place on the

Duke's yacht a few months ago. The whole thing seems to be casting doubt on the state of the Queen's marriage."

"That Duke of Edinburgh," Miguel jested. "Such a roustabout!"

Rosa punched his shoulder. She guessed that Miguel knew little, nor cared much, about the affairs of the Royal Family. "For goodness' sake, don't let anyone hear you say that!" Rosa glanced around the crowded train.

"We'll have to settle with having lunch with Winston Churchill, I guess," Miguel said with a faux sigh. Then, turning back to the serious matter at hand, he said, "I've been thinking. It seems like the original police investigation largely centered around someone who might have a vendetta against Winston. Am I right?"

"Yes, that's largely true."

"Now there's this Joan Freeman lady, who seems to have had some sort of hostility toward not only Winston but Vivien as well."

"We should talk to her," Rosa said. "But are you thinking there might be others?"

Miguel shrugged. "It's possible, isn't it? How much of that angle was discussed in fifty-one?"

"Vivien was very well regarded," Rosa said. "She'd

almost finished her training as a solicitor, something, as you know, that's a rare thing for a lady. She possessed wit and determination, yet was also very likable and kind."

Rosa sighed. "To be honest, I couldn't find one person willing to say anything negative about her. None of her fellow students at the university, none of her friends. That's why it was so shocking to hear Joan Freeman talk about her like that."

"Was she seeing anyone at the time?" Miguel asked.

"Yes. She dated a man named Gerald Withers for a while. It hadn't got all that serious, but she had gone out with him a few times. He was a junior partner in a firm of solicitors called Withers and Bannon, started by Gerald's father. In fact, I remember something about Vivien hoping to get a position there."

"Were they still seeing each other when Vivien died?"

"Yes. The police questioned him. I questioned him myself."

"And?"

"According to Mr. Withers, he and Vivien were on good terms with one another when the murder happened. He was away on a fishing trip that night, somewhere in Scotland, if I remember rightly. His office staff confirmed it. His picture is on the wall that I showed you. Just another dead end."

"Do you think it's worth looking him up again?"

"I don't know, but I think Joan Freeman is a priority." Rosa leaned back in her seat as the train slowed for the next station. "Though she could just be a bitter woman spouting off after a few drinks."

"Yes, she could be," Miguel said. "But let's see it through anyway. Didn't Miss Waldren say Miss Freeman worked at the same hotel?"

Rosa grabbed Miguel's hand and kissed his cheek. She was once again very thankful to have brought him along.

CHAPTER 10

*R*osa and Miguel walked up the crowded cemented stairway at Piccadilly Circus tube station, onto the busy walkway, and over to the corner of Shaftesbury Avenue and Coventry Street. With a note of awe at the density of the population, Miguel said, "And I thought Los Angeles was congested."

Located just a few buildings down on Coventry Street, The Burlington was a brand-new, four-story hotel that had been obviously built to cater to the upper-class crowd. Although modern and clean-looking, it blended perfectly with the other older buildings in the area, all being made of ornate white stone. Ornamental wrought-iron railings adorned the balconies, which served each one of the rooms on every level.

Debbie Waldren stood at the reception desk and smiled when she saw them approach. She had a brass name tag pinned to her uniform.

"We're hoping to have a quick word with Miss Freeman," Rosa explained.

"I see." A look of hesitancy crossed Miss Waldren's face. Was she about to make an excuse? Perhaps she was worried about her job position, but then she seemed to change her mind, and directed them to Joan Freeman's office, which was tucked away at the end of the east hallway on the third floor. The door, which was left half-open, had a HOUSEKEEPING sign attached to it.

Joan Freeman wore a light wool dress suit with a pencil skirt that ended mid-shin. Gaping pockets adorned the hips. She sat at a table, bent over a small stack of papers, her legs crossed at the ankles. There were no windows, and on the back wall was a blackboard with a calendar etched onto it. A schedule filled with names and dates was drawn out in chalk.

"Miss Freeman," Rosa called out as she opened the door a little more. "Is that you?"

Miss Freeman looked up in surprise, then scowled. "Hello."

"Do you remember me? From the tavern last night? I thought perhaps with the drinking—"

"Yes, I remember you." She picked up a pen and looked back down at the papers on her desk. "As you can see, I'm rather busy. We have a businessmen's convention starting this afternoon, and two girls have phoned in sick. We also have a washing machine that has chosen to break down today. I really—"

"We just need a few moments of your time," Rosa pressed. "Your manager gave us permission to speak to you." It was a stretch of the truth, but it got the response Rosa was after.

Miss Freeman stilled, her eyebrows narrowing. "Look. I had a few too many last night, and I'm sorry if I said something to offend you. I know that you and Lady Vivien were friendly."

"I'm only after the truth," Rosa said. "If you know something that could help."

Miss Freeman stared at her for a moment, then with a sigh, she took out a notepad from her desk drawer, scribbled something on it, and handed it to Rosa.

"Kingston Automotive?" Rosa asked.

"A man named Clive Blackmore once managed it. Perhaps he's still there."

Rosa and Miguel shared a look. That was the second time they'd heard that name.

"Why do we want to talk to him?" Miguel asked.

As if she were reluctant to say more, Miss Freeman's mouth formed into a thin line. She glanced between them before saying, "Actually, he might not even be in London anymore. I have no idea. I just know he worked there for a few years.

"Why are you giving this to us?" Miguel looked her in the eyes.

"He was soft on Lady Vivien for months before she died. Doesn't make him a killer, but he might know something that can help you."

"Lady Vivien never mentioned him to me," Rosa said. "In fact, she was seeing someone else at the time."

"Yes, I know.," Miss Freeman acknowledged. "That makes it even worse to be sending the wrong message to Mr. Blackmore like that."

"What makes you believe she was sending the wrong message?" Rosa asked.

"He told me how she was always flirting and carrying on with him."

Rosa could not fathom that being true. It was so unlike the Vivien she had known from childhood.

And had Vivien been interested in Mr. Blackmore, Rosa was sure she would've confided in her.

"Besides," Miss Freeman leaned forward as if she were about to say something conspiratorial. "It wasn't all roses and chocolates between Lady Vivien and that solicitor she was seeing."

Surprised by this accusation, Rosa asked, "How do you know that?"

Miss Freeman smirked. "She told Mr. Blackmore. That's what gave him hope that he had a chance with her. She had big regrets about the fella she was seeing and was getting more and more friendly with poor Mr. Blackmore."

"What did you mean when you said some burglars are not really burglars?" Miguel asked. "Do you think this Mr. Blackmore fellow could have followed her home?"

Miss Freeman glanced away. "I don't know what I meant by saying that. My friends will tell you that I talk nonsense starting around my third glass."

"Do you remember attacking Winston Eveleigh with a paring knife?" Rosa asked.

Joan Freeman burst out laughing. The sound of it was boisterous and unforced. The woman obviously found the question genuinely funny.

"Did he tell you that? Blimey, that's ancient history. Lord Winston approached me in a restaurant lounge one night. We saw each other once more, but I found him a little too quick with his hands, if you get my meaning. I got the feeling he was only interested in one thing, so I broke it off, and that was that. Lord or not, I don't tolerate being treated like a tart. He would've abandoned me the next morning, I'm sure."

"So there was no paring knife?" Rosa asked.

"Nothing of the sort! I could tell he was miffed, but there was no knife and no attack."

"That's a very different version to what he told us," Miguel said.

"Is it now? But really, I don't care. Like I said, ancient history."

"Where were you on the night of Vivien's death?" Miguel asked.

Miss Freeman flashed a haughty look. "Visiting my mum in Cornwall." She turned to Rosa, furrowing her brows. "That's a question police usually ask someone who is a suspect. I hope you don't think I killed Lady Vivien!"

"Just dotting the i's and crossing the t's," Rosa said.

Miss Freeman snorted. "Now, if you don't mind, I'm really very busy."

"Thank you for your time, Miss Freeman," Rosa said.

As Rosa and Miguel entered the lift, Miguel asked, "What do you think about her story about her and Winston?"

"It's hard to say."

"You know him well," Miguel said as the lift descended. "Would he behave that way with a woman?"

"I'm afraid in my early days with Winston, I wore rose-colored glasses. But now, well, I've seen a rather distasteful side to him."

Miguel frowned. "Was he ever rough with you?"

The lift hit the ground floor, and Rosa waited for the doors to open. "No, well—"

"Well?" Miguel prompted tersely.

"There was one time, but he'd had a lot to drink, and it wasn't an attack. He just grabbed my arm and wouldn't let go."

It had left bruises, but he'd apologized profusely the following day, and he'd never manhandled her again after that.

"That cad!" Miguel spat.

Rosa had to agree. "I suppose I wouldn't put it past him to look at someone like Joan Freeman, someone in a lower social class, as a woman to be used and then discarded. I wouldn't have said that when we first started dating, but—"

"I do," Miguel said suddenly, catching Rosa off guard.

"You do what?"

"I *do* think Joan Freeman could be on our list of suspects."

Rosa had to agree. "She did seem awfully keen on steering us away from her conflict with Winston."

It was late afternoon by the time Rosa and Miguel entered the office building where Withers and Bannon was located. Because of their recent travel through the time zones, they had both found themselves ravenously hungry after meeting with Joan Freeman. Fortunately, there was a wonderful Indian restaurant humorously named Kipling's Regret in the neighborhood that served early suppers. Rosa could smell curry spice on their clothes and hoped the tiny mint-flavored tablets that the restaurant kept in a bowl for the customers were up to the task of masking their breath.

"It's okay if we both have curry flavor on our breaths," Miguel said as they walked toward the lift. "That way, when we kiss, it serves as the memory of a good meal, instead of just an embarrassing moment."

"You're so romantic," Rosa said as she pushed the button.

After finding the right door at the end of the wide, carpeted hallway, they entered a reception area, where a young woman sat behind a wooden counter, talking on the telephone. A brass sign with the firm of solicitors' name written in bold lettering hung on the wall behind her. As they approached the desk, the receptionist ended the call.

"Welcome to Withers and Bannon. Do you have an appointment?" she politely said as she hung up the receiver.

"I'm afraid we don't," Rosa said. "I'm an old friend of Mr. Gerald Withers visiting from America. As we were in the area, I suggested we should call in and say hello."

Miguel played along. "We should have called ahead."

The receptionist flicked her long painted finger-nails. "You're in luck! Gerald has just returned from an appointment."

Rosa thought it odd that an office receptionist would call her employer by his first name. Then she noticed a wedding ring on her left ring finger.

"Who shall I say is calling?" The woman turned to an intercom system beside her on the counter.

"Please tell him Rosa Reed is here."

"Very good," she said and then pressed a button on her intercom. Rosa could hear a staticky but familiar voice on the other end, *"Jolly good! What a pleasant surprise! Please do send her in."*

Gerald Withers had changed little since the last time Rosa had seen him over six years earlier. Now in his late thirties, he remained youthful-looking and attractive. He wore a white-silk, collared shirt with a black tie, black trousers, and leather shoes shined to perfection. His brown hair, now showing hints of gray at the temples, was slicked and parted at the side. Rosa detected the faint smell of expensive cologne as he rose from his fancy walnut desk and crossed the room to shake hands.

"Rosa Reed! How wonderful. I haven't seen you since . . . well, since the funeral."

"It's good to see you, Gerald. This is Detective Miguel Belmonte from the Santa Bonita Police." She grasped Miguel's arm and squeezed it to indicate their relationship.

Gerald smiled at Miguel and shook his hand heartily. "Welcome, Detective." He gestured to the plush leather chairs facing his desk. "Santa Bonita, eh? That sounds like it's somewhere even further west than Cardiff!" He chuckled as he turned to take his office chair.

Rosa took an appreciative look around the office. She'd spared no expense at her own office in Santa Bonita, having installed a darkroom, a kitchenette, and a small library, but Gerald Withers' office was the very definition of the word "posh." The thickly carpeted room featured an expansive view overlooking the Thames through wide windows that went almost from ceiling to floor. In the distance, one could see Tower Bridge.

"I heard that you had moved to America," Gerald said. "Good for you. Are you working there?"

"Yes, I have my own investigative office."

"Wonderful. Of course, you do. And you no doubt work with this handsome fellow from time to time." He smiled again at Miguel.

"Yes, we've worked on a few cases together," Miguel said. "It's a small city, so our paths tend to cross often."

"You've done well for yourself, haven't you?" Rosa said with a nod of her chin. "As I recall, you were a junior partner before."

"That's true. My father passed away in fifty-two, and since then, I have been more or less captain of the ship. Mr. Bannon is semi-retired now. We have fourteen employees and several other offices on this floor alone. That's my wife, Linda, out there at reception. We've been married for almost a year. She insists on keeping her job at the firm until the children come. I have no problems with that." He smiled. "I like having her around."

He glanced at Rosa's left hand, her fingers thankfully covered by her gloves, but she caught the inference: *Was she married?*

She didn't take the bait. "I'm delighted for you, Gerald."

"Thank you. Yes. We're quite happy. But what about you? What could possibly drag you both away from the sun-drenched vistas of California to rainy England?"

"We came to visit my parents, but I'm afraid there's another reason, and it's why we decided to drop in to see you at such short notice."

Gerald cocked his head to one side. "Oh?"

"Scotland Yard contacted my parents," Rosa said. "The police thought there was a recent break in Lady Vivien Eveleigh's case."

Rosa watched as the amiable expression on Gerald Withers' face grew serious.

"I see. Have they caught the killer? I haven't heard anything."

"No, they haven't." Rosa shook her head. "The lead they thought they had has turned out to be less than solid."

"I'm very sorry to hear it."

Rosa took a deep breath. "But there are some other things. Things that didn't come up during the initial investigation that I just want to check on."

Gerald Withers' eyebrows came together. "Like what?"

"Well, it could be nothing, but we've been told things were not going well between you and Vivien when she died. To my memory, that's not true. Vivien never mentioned anything like that to me, and we were quite close, as I'm sure you recall. I just wonder why this person would say such a thing."

Gerald Withers scowled. "What a strange thing to say. I mean, after all these years. Who is this person?"

"Her name is Joan Freeman. She was studying law with Vivien."

"I'm afraid I don't know that name."

"It could be that you never met her. I only met her once in passing."

"Then why—?"

"Maybe Miss Freeman knows something, and

she's trying to mislead us," Miguel offered, "wanting to throw us off the real trail."

Gerald looked at Miguel for a moment, then nodded. "Yes, I suppose that could be the case. But I don't have a clue as to what this Miss Freeman is insinuating. Lady Vivien and I had only been seeing each other for three months—it feels like a blip in time now—but as far as I was concerned, we were starting to fall in love. I didn't know her as long as you did, Rosa, but her death hit me very hard. I can't tell you how much I regret being away when it happened."

"You mustn't blame yourself," Rosa said. "Even if you'd been at home, you couldn't have prevented it."

"I suppose that's true, but I still can't help wishing I hadn't gone on that blasted fishing trip!"

Rosa sympathized. "There's no use beating yourself up over that, Gerald. I have regrets, too, but healing begins with forgiving oneself first. I'm just learning that."

Gerald Withers folded his hands together on his desk. "I do hope you can catch the killer, although it seems to me to be a rather remote possibility after all these years."

He shifted and got to his feet, indicating the end

of the conversation, and Rosa and Miguel stood as well.

"It was good to see you again," Rosa said with a smile. "I'm so pleased to see you're doing well."

"Good to see you too," Mr. Withers said. "I wish you well in your ventures."

Just as they were about to leave, Miguel spun on his heel. "Just one question, Mr. Withers. I'm a long-time sport fisherman—"

Rosa glanced at him in surprise. This was news to her.

Miguel continued, "I have this crazy idea that I might want to make a trip up to Scotland while I'm here. Where is it that you like to go?"

"I go angling on the Isle of Arran," Mr. Withers said without hesitation. "This is the perfect time of year for it. Loch Gabard is fabulous."

"Sounds interesting."

"Here, let me write it down for you." Gerald grabbed a pen off his desk, jotted the information down on a pad of paper, ripped the page off its pad, and then handed it to Miguel. "I hire a cottage from an estate agent called Barrymore Estates. That's the telephone number. They know me well. Just mention my name. I always say, 'There's nothing better than fresh rainbow trout in the pan with a square of melting butter.'"

"So true," Miguel said. "Hey, thank you for this! That's great. How many times have you been there?"

"I've been going since my dad took me there as a teenager. I've never bothered going anywhere else. Once you've found heaven, why go looking for a better spot?"

Rosa watched Miguel with admiration. A very clever way to establish Gerald Withers' alibi.

"And here I thought you were just another pretty face," Rosa said as they stepped alone into the lift.

Miguel smirked, rewarding Rosa with the appearance of his beautiful dimples. "I think you're confusing me with Ricky Ricardo. Sanchez does that, too, all the time."

"Do you even like to eat fish?" Rosa asked.

Miguel made a face. "I would rather swallow crushed glass."

CHAPTER 11

*R*osa and Miguel had just finished a late breakfast when Ginger walked into the morning room, fashionably dressed in day dress with a full pleated skirt printed in a bold geometric design. It had sleeves that cuffed at the elbows and a narrow belt made of the same fabric. A short strand of pearls sitting close to her mother's neck emphasized her sophistication.

"You two are late to the breakfast table today," she said as she sat beside her daughter.

"I know." Rosa wiped her mouth with a napkin. "Still a bit on California time."

Ginger dangled a set of keys in front of Rosa. "This might wake you up, love."

Rosa smiled, took the keys, and then looked

across the table at Miguel sipping his coffee. "You thought my corvette was the bee's knees. Wait until you see this baby!"

Miguel's eyes widened. "I don't know whether to be excited or frightened."

"A little bit of *both* is what I find to be the best mixture for a motorcar ride in the country on a beautiful day," Ginger said. "You're welcome to give it a go, too, you know."

"Thank you, but not until you Brits catch on to the idea of driving on the correct side of the road."

"I heard that!" came Basil's indignant voice.

"He likes to read the morning paper in his office which is conveniently next to the breakfast room and also the kitchen, and also, close to the tin in the pantry which holds the cake." Ginger looked amusedly at Miguel's sheepish expression. "Anyway, it has to do with the sword hand."

"The sword hand?" Miguel said.

"Yes, driving on the left side of the road goes back to medieval times. When traveling on dangerous roads on your horse or in your carriage, you could fend off attackers with your sword or pitchfork or whatever you had in your right hand. Most people are right-handed; that was true back then as well."

"Let me get this straight," Rosa said as she stared at Miguel. "I have to do the driving *and* fend off road bandits with a sword? What are you going to do?"

Miguel cocked his head. "Hold on for dear life, I imagine. I'm glad to know why the English have a fascination with the left of things."

"Thanks, Mum," Rosa said. "I promise we'll get the MG back to you in good shape." She finished her tea, but her mind had drifted to what Miguel had just said. *The left of things.*

"Come with me," she said to Miguel as she sprung to her feet.

"I thought that was the plan the whole time."

"I mean to the attic where I have the case room."

"Sure," Miguel said, following Rosa up the staircase. "But you'll have to explain to me why I'm chasing you."

Rosa turned the lights on in the case room, stared at the board, then grabbed the thin decorative cushion from the chair. She stared at Miguel's shoes.

"I need a shoelace."

"What?"

"Humor me. Let me borrow one of your laces."

"Okay." Miguel lowered himself, untied his right shoe, and handed the black lace to Rosa. She folded the cushion into a tube shape and tied it with the lace.

"This is roughly the size of a lady's neck, wouldn't you say?" Rosa said. "I mean, it's a bit longer, but the girth is about right."

"I suppose," Miguel said warily.

She held the cushion tube out toward him. "Now, I want you to pretend that you are strangling someone."

Miguel's mouth dropped open, then closed. "Fine." He grabbed the cushion and squeezed while Rosa observed his grip.

"Yes, now do it again," she said.

Miguel repeated the move.

"All right, now do it six more times, take a step back, and then forward quickly like you're attacking."

"I want to go on record that I harbor no ill will toward this innocent furniture accessory," Miguel said.

"Duly noted. Now go ahead and strangle the vile thing."

Miguel did as instructed.

"Now, one more time." She wiggled the cushion in front of his face. "It's still alive!"

"Dang pillow!" Miguel said with a grunt. "There."

He handed the cushion back to Rosa. "No cushion could have survived that onslaught. Do you have anything else I can brutalize? Perhaps an old towel or a balled-up bedsheet that deserves retributive justice?"

"You grabbed it the same way every time," Rosa said.

"I did?"

"Take it again." Rosa handed the cushion back to Miguel, who grabbed it with both hands, encircling it with his fingers.

"Look at where your thumbs are," she instructed.

His right thumb was higher on the cushion than his left. They overlapped by about an inch.

"I'm right-handed," Miguel said. "The dominant thumb goes above every time." He turned and pointed his chin toward the wall board. They both walked toward it, eyes fixed on the picture of Vivien's neck.

"But not like the killer," Rosa said. The top contour of the bruises on the front of Vivien's neck formed visible lines where two thumbs overlapped each other, the left over the right. The killer had choked Vivien with his thumbs pressed against her windpipe. Rear and side photos taken at the morgue and pinned next to the other photos on the wall showed bruises from eight fingers on the back and side of her neck.

"Forensic analysis determined the approximate size of the hands and the angle of the grip," Rosa said, "but no one thought about the overlapping thumbs and how they would indicate which hand was dominant. I mean, it's not conclusive, of course, but it *is* a powerful indicator that the killer is likely to be left-handed." Rosa bit her lip. "Now we just have to interview everyone in London who is left-handed and around five foot eight. How hard can that be?"

"It does narrow it down somewhat," Miguel said. "I read somewhere that only around ten percent of the world's population are left-handed."

"In that case, we should have this whole thing wrapped up by teatime."

"At any rate, we do have a good head start already."

"What do you mean?" Rosa asked.

"Joan Freeman is left-handed."

"You noticed that?"

"She wrote down the name of that car dealership with her left hand. *But* so did Gerald Withers when he handed me the name of the cabin leasing company."

"Interesting," Rosa said. "However, he was away. I also have very little reason to doubt him about the state of his relationship with Vivien at the time. Joan Freeman's word on it is suspect, to say the least."

"No motive, no history of violence that we know of, and a good alibi but . . ." Miguel held up the note that Gerald Withers had given him. "It would be nice to make sure."

"I'll ring them. I need a cover story of some kind," Rosa said. "They're probably not going to give out that information freely, and I don't want to cast any suspicion on Gerald by saying I'm with the police. That is his favorite fishing spot, after all."

"Why don't I try," Miguel said. "I have an idea."

The nearest telephone connection was in the library, one floor down. Rosa sat in one of the wing-back chairs while Miguel made the call. Rosa leaned in close so she could hear both sides of the conversation.

"Good afternoon, this is the office of Barrymore Estates and Holdings. How may I help you?" The voice was female and held the hint of a Scottish brogue.

"Good afternoon to you, or . . . morning where I am, I should say." Miguel chuckled. "My name is Hernandez." He winked at Rosa who had one eyebrow raised. "I'm phoning from the editorial office of *Fishing and Wildlife* magazine in Los Angeles. We are doing a piece on famous fishing locations in Scotland, and I would like to talk to someone about your place by Loch Gabard."

"Oh, that's a wonderful wee spot," came the response. "My name is Mrs. Kirk, and I can help you with that. I'm in charge of bookings and the like. Mr. Kirk and I love to go there when we can. Los Angeles! My, my! I had no idea we were even known outside the British Isles."

"Well, here's the thing," Miguel continued. "It really only came to the attention of our editorial department because of a fellow who used to work here. His name is Matt Conners. Now he was, unfortunately . . . um . . . let go a few months ago. He wrote a few too many tall tales about the fishing trips the magazine sent him on. We began to suspect he wasn't really going to those places. He also claimed to have met with high-ranking officials, movie stars, and even well-known judges and lawyers.

"After a while, we started to suspect a lot of that was a bunch of hooey. He never took pictures of any of those people, had no proof. Now, the magazine *did* send him to Scotland in 1951, and from . . . um

. . . let me check a minute." He covered up the receiver and whispered to Rosa, "Exactly when did the murder take place?"

"March the fourteenth."

Miguel continued his charade. "From March twelfth to March eighteenth, he was supposed to have been at Loch Gabard on the Isle of Arran, but we strongly suspect he wasn't fishing at all. His details on the place were very vague. We think he was actually in Glasgow at a . . . bagpipers' convention." Miguel winced at his own words.

Rosa's eyebrows came together in bafflement.

"A pipers' convention?" Mrs. Kirk said. "I don't know if I've ever heard of such a thing."

"I think it's mostly American ex-pats who go to those types of things. Fellows who have a fascination for Scottish music. It's probably not at all popular with the locals."

Rosa rolled her eyes.

"Anyway," Miguel continued. "I know we're behind on this since that was a few years ago, but we are very backed up here at the magazine. We have the piece he did on Loch Gabard, but we want to make sure we have the facts straight before we publish it."

"All right," Mrs. Kirk said. "Whatever I can do to help."

"Conners told us that a very high-profile lawyer from London comes there often and that he and Conners spent a lot of time together on that trip. Conners bragged about it quite a bit in his manuscript. The lawyer's name is Gerald Withers."

"Oh, of course, we know Mr. Withers. He comes here almost every year and has for a long time. I had no idea he was so well known."

"Oh yeah, he has an excellent reputation. Kind of a fast-rising star in the whole litigation scene in London."

Rosa frowned again.

"Do you have records that go back that far to see if Conners was even there on that date with Mr. Withers?" Miguel asked.

"I think so, just a moment." Rosa could hear Mrs. Kirk opening a filing cabinet and rifling through some files. "All right. I have the file from that month. Now let's see . . . hmm." There was a moment's pause. "That's odd."

"Conners wasn't there, was he?" Miguel said. "I knew it."

"No, he wasn't. In fact, neither was Mr. Withers."

"What? You're sure?" Miguel looked at Rosa.

"Yes, I am. And now that you mention it, I seem to remember Mr. Withers not coming at all that year. It's the only year in the last many years that he didn't make a booking with us."

Miguel thanked her and hung up the phone. They returned to the case room to stare at the image of Vivien Eveleigh's fallen body.

CHAPTER 12

The next day, the sun wasn't quite warm enough to drive with the top down, but the sunshine did help to make the ninety-minute drive northeast to Essex and the town of Chelmsford a pleasant one.

"Everything is so green," Miguel commented at the rolling pastures and woodlands. "I imagine this is where Robin Hood and his gang used to hang out, right?"

"You're thinking of Sherwood Forest," Rosa said, "which is farther north. But perhaps if he had a car like this he might have roamed further south on a nice day like today."

"Yeah, just Robin and Friar Tuck taking a day off

from robbing the rich to go drag the main in old London town."

Rosa cocked a brow as she glanced at Miguel. "Drag the main?"

"Cruise up and down Main Street looking for . . . *birds*, I guess they call them here."

"A proper friar would never engage in such activities."

The MG Roadster hugged the road like a long-lost friend, its engine thrumming contentedly underneath the hood. Rosa drove at a leisurely pace, although she was sure she could have driven much faster and still easily negotiated the winding highway.

They reached the outskirts of Chelmsford just after 2 p.m. Miguel pulled out the map on which Rosa had circled the address in blue ink. They had passed several lots where construction fences had been erected. One could see through the wires to rows of twisted concrete and rubble beyond.

"Looks like they tore down some old buildings," Miguel observed.

"Those buildings weren't torn down so much as bombed," Rosa said. "This town was heavily hit by the Luftwaffe in the spring of forty-three. Fourteen years later, they're still rebuilding."

"Wow," Miguel whistled. "We're a long way from California."

It took another half hour to find Kingston Automotive situated close to the heart of Chelmsford. It was doing a booming business, as Rosa estimated at least seventy cars, of varying makes and ages, parked on the lot. Colorful ribbons and banners hung all over the lot, advertising special deals and prices for the week.

Rosa parked the MG beside an older model Ford that had been polished and shined to perfection. The sign on the window read, "Drive it home today for £300."

There was a large redbrick, ground-level building with the word "OFFICE" painted over the front double-door entrance. It didn't take long before a man in a black suit and tie emerged from the building and started toward them. The building had been fitted with an abundance of windows to let the salesmen know when someone had come onto the lot. These places often relied on walk-in clients, those who had no appointments but just wanted to "kick the tires" in search of a potential deal.

Rosa had called ahead to ask if Clive Blackmore still worked at the lot and was told he would be there today. She didn't know if she'd ever met him in passing and wondered if she would recognize him. Vivien had never mentioned him to her, and she half wondered if Joan Freeman had made the whole thing up.

But she didn't have to search the grounds to find Mr. Blackmore. His voice bellowed across the lot. "I can't believe it. Miss Rosa Reed!" he offered with a stunned look on his face.

In his early thirties, the man had a stocky build and was about five foot eight inches tall. His pronounced nose looked like it had been broken at least once or twice, and his wide and deep-set eyes were framed with heavy eyebrows. These features, along with his brown bowler hat, gave him a brutish look. Rosa could imagine him starring in a gangster film at home.

"I think you have me at a disadvantage," Rosa said.

The man walked over and extended his right hand. "Clive Blackmore, at your service."

Rosa and Miguel both feigned ignorance of the name.

"I was a friend of Lady Vivien Eveleigh," he said, then gaped in disbelief. "You mean you don't remember me?"

"Oh, well, you *do* look a bit familiar now that you

mention it," Rosa said, stretching the truth. She didn't remember seeing this man, and he had a face that one wouldn't easily forget.

Rosa gestured to Miguel. "This is Miguel Belmonte, visiting from California."

Miguel extended his right hand. "Hello, good to meet you."

"My pleasure," Mr. Blackmore replied. He turned his attention to the MG and whistled. "That's certainly a beauty you're driving there, isn't it? I hope you're thinking of trading her in today. I could sell it over again in a minute." He winked at Rosa.

Rosa placed a gloved finger on her chin. "I don't think so, not today." She nodded at Miguel. "We were driving through Chelmsford on the way to Clacton-on-Sea to see some old friends, and we spied a few interesting cars on your forecourt. Mr. Belmonte is quite a car enthusiast, and I was boasting about the makes and models we have in England that aren't available in America. Who knows? If he likes something, perhaps he'll purchase it and keep it in Kensington for the time being."

The mention of Kensington was deliberate. It was well known to be a pricey place to live, and that, along with the MG, gave the impression of wealth, a notion that played well to the car salesman. Rosa and

Miguel had discussed it and had decided not to let Clive Blackmore know that they were investigating him, at least not at first. Instead, they would give the impression that Rosa had returned to London. That way, his attention would be focused on them as a potential big sale, and he'd relax with easy chatter. Private investigators had more freedom than the police in this regard. They didn't have to reveal they were working on a case.

The plan was for Miguel to be looking for a car, while Rosa would engage Clive in conversation about Vivien.

"Oh, how fortuitous that I'm the chap who gets to help you then." His strange smile was vaguely off-putting, and Rosa wondered how successful he was at sales. An image of a fox posing as a feed salesman at a chicken farm crossed her mind.

Miguel scanned the lot. "For starters, I'd like to take a look at that coupe over there." He nodded toward a red, rather boxy-looking convertible with a leather interior.

"That's a 1954 Austin Somerset A40 Coupe," Clive said as they slowly walked toward it. "Low mileage."

The next ten minutes were spent talking about the car's attributes. Miguel did a good job appearing interested as he sat in the driver's seat and asked questions, but in the end, made it clear that the car wasn't for him and that he might browse a bit more.

"Of course, be my guest." Clive waved his hand to indicate the lot was all his to peruse.

"So, how long did you know Lady Vivien?" Rosa asked as she and Clive slowly walked side by side as Miguel went on ahead.

"We were very close for a long time," Clive said wistfully.

Rosa doubted that very much. "Is that so? How did you meet?"

"I met her at the British Museum, of all places. We were both looking through the exhibition on the destruction of Pompeii. I have a fascination for Roman history. Anyway, we just sort of struck up a conversation that soon turned into a friendship."

Rosa remembered that Vivien did like to go to the British Museum and was a history enthusiast. Rosa had accompanied her on occasion.

"We weren't in a romantic relationship really," Mr. Blackmore said, "although I always got the feeling she would have been interested if I had been."

"I see," Rosa said, not believing it for a second. "I only remember a fellow by the name of Gerald Withers."

Mr. Blackmore's expression tightened. "Lady Vivien told me about Mr. Withers. They had a terrible argument about a week before she died. It was at a colleague's birthday party, and Mr. Withers stormed out, leaving Lady Vivien in tears. She thought she must've embarrassed him in some way, although she didn't know how exactly."

"Oh, that's interesting," Rosa said. "She didn't mention that event to me."

"No? Well, in a way, that's not really surprising. She tended to share things with me that she didn't with others. Now, I don't know the exact details. As you know, she was reticent to speak ill of anyone. But she was quite upset by it. She came to me looking for consolation afterwards . . ." He let the sentence hang.

Rosa had a strange feeling about this man. The word "creepy" came to mind.

"I'll never forget when I heard the news about her death, nearly choked on my toast when I read the morning paper," Rosa stated. "I was devastated, of course. What about you, Mr. Blackmore? Were you in London at the time?"

It was a roundabout way of asking the question, "Where were you on the night of—"

As far as Rosa knew, Clive Blackmore had never

been questioned by the police. In fact, no one had drawn any connection between Vivien and him at that time, which was strange considering his claim they were such close friends.

"No, I was here in Chelmsford," Mr. Blackmore claimed. "As I recall, I was at home with a cold that night."

Over six years later, it would be nearly impossible to check his alibi.

"By the way, how's Lord Winston faring?" he asked. "I lost track of him after Lady Vivien died."

Rosa cast the salesman a curious glance. Winston would hardly spend time with a man who sold cars for a living, much less condone a relationship involving his sister.

"I really couldn't say."

Mr. Blackmore removed a package of cigarettes from his shirt pocket. He offered one to Rosa and then picked one out for himself after she declined. While he struck a match to light his smoke, he stopped walking for a moment, then continued, "I think he berated her a lot because of, you know, her early weight problems."

A sudden chill went through Rosa. How on earth did this man know about *that*?

CHAPTER 13

"*D*id you notice he was left-handed?"

Rosa and Miguel climbed back into the MG, and Rosa signaled to turn onto the main road. She continued. "I watched him light a cigarette, definitely left-handed."

"Seems like there are a lot of lefties on this island," Miguel said. "Blackmore's built like he could strangle somebody too. A sturdy guy, if not gullible. I convinced him I wanted an Aston Martin coupe and gave him a fake number to call should one show up for sale on the lot. He told me that he would drive into the town of Colchester tonight to talk to the manager of an affiliated motorcar lot." He chuckled. "I could almost see the dollar signs in his eyes as he thought about the commission."

"Pound signs."

"Yeah, right, pound signs. Doesn't quite have the same ring to it." He looked at Rosa, his brows furrowing. "Is something wrong?"

"He knows a detail about Vivien that he shouldn't," Rosa said. "She was a very private person and never spoke about certain things to anyone except her very closest friends; her inner circle was very small. In fact, during the years following the death of her parents, I think I was her only *real* confidante."

"What does Blackmore know?" Miguel asked.

Rosa shifted into a lower gear and then slowed the car to a stop beside the curb on one of the less busy streets in the town and turned to Miguel. "When Vivien was a child, she was rather pudgy; some would even say obese. At first, the doctors said it was a glandular problem. They tried treating her, but nothing helped. However, when she started puberty, the extra weight just fell off. The doctors chalked it all up to hormonal imbalance but couldn't pinpoint more than that. She found the whole affair extremely embarrassing and never liked to talk about it, especially with a member of the opposite sex."

Miguel shared Rosa's alarm. "And Blackmore knew this about her?"

"Yes. Oddly, he managed to work it into our conversation."

"How would a guy like that get information of that sort?"

"That's the mystery," Rosa said. "Only Winston and I are privy to Vivien's health history."

"No childhood pictures?"

"She destroyed all but one as a reminder to never let herself get that way again if she could help it. She kept it at the bottom of the drawer where she kept her undergarments."

There was a moment of silence as Rosa and Miguel read a white, painted menu board on the pavement in front of a restaurant. Miguel nodded slowly, raised his eyebrows, and looked at Rosa as if this were some preordained, fate-filled moment. "Fish pie?"

"You don't eat fish."

"True. I'm just wondering what type of person would put fish in a pie." He grinned. "You can have that if you want. I'm suggesting we stop for a bite."

"All right. I'm getting hungry too." She batted her eyes. "You're sure you don't want to try the fish pie?"

"I'll stick to the steak and ale thank you very

much." He smirked and then looked at his watch. "The car lot closes at five, which means we have about ninety minutes to discuss how we'll search that strange man's apartment after we follow him home. We already know he is going out to find me an Aston Martin. How far away is Colchester?"

"About an hour."

"That gives at least two hours. Fabulous."

"You don't mind being arrested for unlawful entry, should we get caught?" Rosa teased. "Things could look bad for you, as a foreigner."

"That's something we can talk about *after* I get some food in me. Besides, how bad could a British jail be anyways?"

"I don't imagine they are pleasant," Rosa said as they stepped out of the MG. "You'd better enjoy your steak and ale while you can."

Miguel wrinkled his nose. "If the police come, I'll probably just run, let you take the fall." He took Rosa's hand as they walked toward the front door of the restaurant. "Your dad has some pull, right."

"Not so much, now that he's retired." Rosa stepped inside as Miguel held the door. "But I'm sure my parents would visit me at weekends."

. . .

CLIVE BLACKMORE LIVED in a small terraced home just on the southern outskirts of Chelmsford. Rosa and Miguel had taken great care to make sure he didn't realize he was being followed; not a simple task considering the car they were driving, but Rosa was confident that, with their combined skills at tailing suspects, they had remained undetected. Across from the row of redbrick townhouses where Mr. Blackmore lived, hedges in a wooded park area provided partial obscurity. From there, Rosa and Miguel could discreetly observe their suspect entering his residence.

"Now we'll have to wait until he leaves," Miguel said, looking again at his watch. "Shouldn't be too long. I got the feeling he was quite keen on finding that expensive Aston Martin for me."

Rosa chuckled. "You're too good at this."

"I've watched a lot of episodes of *Dragnet*. Did you bring your stuff with you?"

Rosa knew what he meant. By now, Miguel expected that wherever she went, Rosa would always have certain items in her handbag. He'd recently referred to it as her "crime-busting kit" because of the lock-picking apparatus, Argus 35 mm camera, small penlight, notepad, and sharpened pencil always found inside. In addition, Rosa often carried a small recording device, which she had purchased a few months earlier, and a Colt .38 snub-nose revolver. The last two items remained in her office in Santa Bonita.

"I have the lockpicks, the penlight, and the camera," she confirmed.

"Cool."

"Don't tell my parents about this," Rosa cautioned. "I've no idea how the former superintendent at Scotland Yard would react if I told him that I'd unlawfully entered someone's private home."

"My lips are sealed," Miguel said, "but I'll bet your mother has employed similar tactics at some time or another."

Rosa thought about that for a moment and had to admit he was probably correct in that assessment. She wasn't sure if that made her feel less uneasy, though.

Miguel was right in his prediction. Twenty-five minutes later, they watched Mr. Blackmore emerge from his house, walk a couple of hundred yards east, and get into the green Vauxhall he had driven home from the car lot.

It was now close to 6:00 p.m., and darkness had comfortably fallen as they cautiously made their way to the back of the bank of terraced houses. The small back garden area was surrounded by a five-foot-high wooden fence that separated each property from its neighbour. Miguel bent down and clenched his hands together to give Rosa a boost. Happy she had worn slacks that day, Rosa touched down as lightly as she could on the other side.

"Thank God he doesn't have a guard dog," she whispered as Miguel rolled himself over the top of the fence and crouched down beside her.

"I thought of that," he said. "That's why I helped you over the fence first." He grinned in the darkness at her.

"And they say chivalry is dead," Rosa murmured as she turned toward the building.

When they reached the ground-floor back entry, Miguel cupped his ear with his hand. "Do you hear that?" he whispered.

"Let me guess. You hear a cat in distress."

"Then you hear it too? We're going to have to break in and help it. It sounds as if it's in great pain."

Rosa sighed, shook her head, and opened her bag. Miguel kept checking the neighbors' windows for onlookers, and Rosa listened for the gears to click as she worked the lock on the door. It only took a moment to disengage it, and soon they were inside.

"I think we should start on the first floor," Rosa

said, still keeping her voice barely above a whisper. "That's likely where more personal things will be found in the bedroom or the study if there is one."

Miguel nodded as they both turned to make their way through the kitchen on the ground level and up a carpeted stairway. The penlight cast just enough of a narrow beam to guide them.

Within a few seconds, they stood in a small, sparsely furnished bedroom. Because they had only one light source, they had to move around the room together, searching under the bed mattress and through the shelves in the nightstand and bureau. Rosa couldn't help but feel the irony of the moment as she suddenly glimpsed herself in a mirror mounted on the vanity. Here they were, rummaging through someone's house like a couple of thieves while on an investigation into someone that had possibly broken into Winston's residence.

Had her desperation to solve this case finally taken her too far? And now she had dragged Miguel into it. Too late now. She slowly blew air out of her cheeks and kept moving.

They searched the entire room, careful not to disturb anything that would lead Clive Blackmore to believe someone had been there. After searching the closet area and under all the furniture, they moved into the other rooms, starting with the bathroom and small office, but found nothing of interest. Rosa searched through Mr. Blackmore's financial records, his photo albums—nothing. The longer they lingered, the guiltier she felt. They had no right nor reason to be rummaging through the salesman's things.

Feeling deflated, Rosa nodded to Miguel to head back downstairs. Since they were already trespassing, they took a moment to search through a small living room area and, last, the kitchen. Finally, Miguel walked over to a door in the short hallway they had passed on the way through the first time.

"If there's anything here at all, I guess this is where we'll find it," Miguel said, twisting the doorknob and stepping out of the way.

They carefully descended a narrow wooden staircase into a musty-smelling cellar. Casting her narrow beam of light, Rosa spied a lone light bulb hanging on the low ceiling with a pull-string to turn it on and off. She motioned for Miguel to close the door at the bottom of the stairway. There were no windows in the cellar, so they could turn on the light having none of it spill out into the back garden.

Momentarily blinded by the blast of light, Rosa and Miguel squinted as their eyes adjusted, staring in surprise at several two-panel, foldable, wood-frame room dividers. The kind schools or hospitals used to partition a larger room into separate smaller spaces temporarily. They were arranged into three cubicles of about five feet in width and two feet in depth. The far wall of the cellar served as the back wall for each one. The dividers were about six feet tall and had a rough wooden counter built against the back, each with a lone wooden chair.

Rosa cast Miguel a questioning look. "Shrines?"

Each counter had several candles along with notes and carefully arranged assorted items like hairbrushes, bracelets, and even some ladies' under-garments. Pieces of parchment paper with what appeared to be two lines of handwritten poetry were pinned to the wall in each cubicle.

All of it was more than strange, but what caught Rosa's attention was the dozens of photographs. On each of the three separated wall spaces were pictures of young women in their early twenties in various posed and unposed shots. Some were snapped as portraits, and some were taken from a distance as if through zoom lenses, with the subjects unaware a picture of them was being taken. All the women were brunettes with similar attractive features. Rosa didn't recognize the young women in the first two cubicles, but there were about a dozen photographs of Vivien Eveleigh in the last one.

Rosa couldn't contain her gasp. One photograph was a copy of another picture Rosa had seen before. Vivien as a pudgy ten-year-old child, the same small picture she had shown Rosa long ago—a night where personal secrets between the two girls were tearfully exchanged. Blackmore must've broken into her living quarters, gone through her things, and snapped a picture.

As her eyes welled up, Rosa put her hand to her mouth to keep from sobbing.

CHAPTER 14

"*L*et's take photographs of everything," Miguel said. "All three cubicles."

Rosa took a shaky breath and nodded as she fumbled with her bag and removed her camera. They began with Vivien's things. There were the same type of items on her wooden counter as on the other two. Besides a dozen pictures, all taken from a distance, was an ivory hair clip, a gold bracelet, some coins placed in a glass dish, and a piece of parchment paper with a poem written on it in careful cursive lettering:

> I am wounded and sorrowed,
> You were here, my love, then gone.
> I guess time was only borrowed

Like a bird's cheering song.
I don't like how it ended,
But every day has its night.
It was not so intended,
But it's all right; it's all right.

As Rosa read the lines, her blood chilled. She took close-ups and shots from further away so one could see all the items together. Next, she moved on to the other "shrines" until her film was used up.

"These items are things that the person might not have missed or assumed they had misplaced," Miguel said. He shook his head and stared at the scene one last time before turning to Rosa. "We got him."

The words went through Rosa like an electric shock. She suddenly felt weak in the knees, and Miguel stepped in to hold her. "It's going to be over soon. We'd better get going before he returns."

As they got back into the MG, Rosa was suddenly overcome with a mix of disgust and anger. Rather than shifting, she rammed the MG into gear and pressed hard on the accelerator. As she rounded the first corner and headed for the main road south, the tires chirped. She hoped a sense of relief would soon replace her rage, but at the moment, all she felt inside was a dark storm.

Miguel seemed to sense this and didn't say a word until twenty miles later. "Let's talk again about how we are going to let the police know."

Over their dinner, they had come up with several scenarios of how they could inform the police in the event they found anything incriminating in Clive Blackmore's house. They had to be inventive, or they'd face criminal charges of unlawful entry, which would only weaken the case against him.

"I think my idea was the best," Rosa said. "After we develop these photographs in my mother's dark-room, we will send them by unmarked special delivery to Scotland Yard. Then I will place a call to their front desk using a disguised voice—I can manage a pretty good Cockney accent. It will be an anonymous tip. I'll tell them that Clive Blackmore took me into his home to stay for a few days and that while he was working at the car dealership, I ventured into the cellar. I'll tell them to expect photographs to confirm what I'm saying and then give them his address.

The pictures should arrive the next day."

"I wonder who the other two ladies are and if they are still alive?" Miguel said. "Poems and notes about them were written in the present tense. Vivien was the only one mentioned in the past tense."

"I hope so, and I expect we'll find out soon. Chief Inspector Fredericks will probably call me as soon as they see the photos and make the arrest."

"I've been thinking about how and why he must have done it," Miguel said. "If the target was Vivien all along and not Winston, that might mean that Vivien could've been murdered in her area of the house, then carried down to Winston's quarters to make it look like a robbery gone wrong."

"That would make sense," Rosa agreed.

"As to motive, well, who knows? The man is unhinged. Anything could have set him off."

"Most likely, he felt spurned by Vivien, and perhaps there was a confrontation earlier that day or week." Rosa shook her head in bewilderment. "I'm just so surprised that I didn't know about him *at all*. I was Vivien's closest friend, and yet, she didn't say a word to me about this man."

"There's the possibility that she didn't actually know him," Miguel said. "Everything he told you at the car lot about his relationship could be nothing more than a delusion in the mind of an unbalanced person. He might've spotted her at the museum and became obsessed. He took those photos of her and the other ladies from a distance. There were pictures of her walking down the street, getting into her car, shopping at the market . . . he must have followed her around for some time. Same thing with those other two women."

It was an awful thing to imagine, having a man following Vivien and taking photographs, stealing into her home, writing poetry . . . all without her knowledge. Rosa's teeth clenched at the thought of it.

By the time they got back to Hartigan House, Rosa's parents had retired for the evening. Rosa had used her mother's darkroom before and knew where all the chemicals and equipment were stored.

Sometime later, she and Miguel stood, staring at the photos hanging on the darkroom drying line, the images gradually growing clearer. When the processing was completed, Rosa was pleased that they had all turned out perfectly and showed details of everything, including all the notes and poems that Clive Blackmore had written.

"He's not exactly Shakespeare," Miguel commented.

When the photographs were dry enough, they cleaned up the darkroom, leaving no traces of the photographs. Rosa didn't like keeping secrets from her parents, partly because they were both so good at uncovering things, but in this case, she didn't want to put them, and her father especially, in an uncomfortable position if she could avoid it. Breaking into someone's house was not a suitable activity for the daughter of a retired police superintendent.

As if Rosa lived in a pleasant dream, the next day passed quickly. She did her best to show Miguel the best London offered and took great comfort in his company during what she found to be an emotionally turbulent time. Miguel was balm for her soul, making her laugh often, as if sensing that levity was what any good doctor would order. He continued to be fascinated by everything English. On his first trip on a double-decker bus, he borrowed Rosa's camera and used up a whole roll of film before they even stepped back onto the street. Rosa purchased several more rolls at a kiosk and resigned herself to letting Miguel be in complete charge of the camera for the duration of their stay in England. It would take days to develop all the shots he took of the theater district, the Royal Albert Hall, Tower Bridge, and Big Ben.

Rosa was also taken with the way Miguel and her parents were getting along. It was so different from the awkward times with Winston. Not only did her father seem taken with Miguel, but he also tried to coerce Miguel into attending another cricket match before it was time to leave London, this time for an entire day.

Not wanting him whisked off for an entire day when they had only a few days left, Rosa warned Miguel off that activity. There were yet things to see and do. *The Mousetrap* was still playing at the Ambassadors Theatre and she was sure Miguel would want to see that.

Or perhaps not, but it would still make for a romantic evening.

THE CALL from Scotland Yard came on the third morning after their covert trip to Chelmsford. Rosa's father had answered the call and announced to Rosa and Miguel over breakfast that Chief Inspector Fredericks would be round in an hour to inform them of a possible recent development in the case.

"He wouldn't go into detail, but it must be something significant if he's going to come over in person to speak to us."

Rosa and Miguel shared a look across the table.

"And here we thought it was all over and done with," Basil Reed went on. "Blast! This case never ends! Let's hope this is at the least the beginning of the end." He looked at Rosa. "He also asked if we could invite Eveleigh over so he could deliver this news to us all at once. I hope that's all right."

Rosa nodded. "Why not?" Under these circumstances, it might be good for them to hear together that the killer had finally been caught. It would give Rosa some satisfaction to watch Winston's reaction, since he so adamantly declared the case was unsolvable.

Rosa and Miguel, along with Ginger and Basil, were sitting together in the sitting room when Collins announced Lord Winston Eveleigh's arrival. As Winston entered the room, the fire roared in the fireplace, but the crackling flames did little to warm the mood. Rosa sensed her father was trying to be cordial, but the way his eyes twitched told her it was forced. He'd never made it a secret that he wasn't fond of Winston. Her mother was a little better at hiding her dislike, but Rosa knew that she, too, had never really bonded with Winston while he and Rosa had been dating.

To Rosa's surprise, she experienced a feeling of empathy for Winston. Rejected by his own father and then publicly by his bride-to-be was a bitter pill. Now that she and Miguel were together, Rosa endeavored to be a little more forgiving of Winston.

Surely, given time, even he would concede there was no longer any possibility of a shared future together.

"I'm glad you are well, Mr. and Mrs. Reed," Winston said. Winston shook hands with Basil and Ginger, then accepted the proffered chair. "This is nice. Everyone together." He focused on Miguel. "Just one big happy family." The smile on his aristocratic face would have seemed genuine to anyone who did not know him well.

Thankfully, Chief Inspector Fredericks arrived shortly afterward. They all sat in a big semicircle on the settees and chairs facing the fire. Ginger offered tea and biscuits, but everyone declined.

"I'd like to just get to the point, if you don't mind," Chief Inspector Fredericks said. He leaned forward in his chair and cleared his throat. "As you know, I've agreed to give you any updates involving the investigation into the murder of Lady Vivien Eveleigh. As it happens, there are three.

"First of all, two days ago, Liverpool police apprehended Jack Corning in an abandoned building near the docks. During questioning, he inadvertently confirmed Mr. Briggs' alibi." Chief Inspector Fredericks scratched his head along the cap line. "Secondly, a witness has been found regarding the poker game Briggs mentioned. An employee of the hotel where the game was played, a bellboy by the name of John Reese, told police he brought drinks to the room at just after midnight on the night in question. He saw the gold cufflink on the table. It doesn't conclusively mean that Briggs didn't steal it from Kenway House, but it lends some credence to his story. Briggs must have forgotten about the bellboy." Letting out a long breath, he added, "Since we don't have any evidence to prove otherwise, it appears that Mr. Briggs had not been to Kenway House on the night of the murder."

"What's the third update?" Rosa asked.

"We received an anonymous tip a few days ago, which was then followed up by an unmarked envelope sent to us via special delivery. The woman who called us claimed to be a recent acquaintance of Clive Blackmore, a car salesman in Chelmsford. She told us she had been staying at his house when she happened upon a strange scene in the cellar. After taking photographs without the owner's knowledge, she sent them to us, and they are now in evidence."

"I don't understand," Winston said.

"The images showed a kind of exhibit involving small personal items, and some handwritten poetry, along with photographs of three different women. One of them was Lady Vivien Eveleigh."

Ginger murmured, "Oh mercy."

Rosa's hand went to her throat. Even though she'd known what the announcement would be, hearing it from the chief inspector's mouth still shocked her. "And the other women?"

"Blackmore had written their names down on various paraphernalia," Chief Inspector Fredericks said. "We didn't have any problems finding them, and thank goodness, they're both alive. Though shaken to discover they had been targeted and followed, neither had any connection with Lady Vivien."

Winston had blanched whiter than fine porcelain. After swallowing with difficulty, he asked, "Have you arrested this devil?"

"Mr. Blackmore has been arrested based on this new evidence." Chief Inspector Fredericks held up a palm. "What's more, he's been arrested for stalking women before. A woman named Miss Stimpson brought charges against him six years ago, and he was convicted and spent time in prison. So this is not the first time we have had the misfortune of hearing the name Clive Blackmore."

"So, we have him!" Winston balled his right hand into a fist and pounded the arm of his chair.

"When will the charge of murder be brought?" Rosa asked, sharing Winston's excitement.

The chief inspector shook his head. "It won't be."

Winston's pale expression moved from white to red with indignation. "Why on earth not?"

"Because Clive Blackmore didn't kill Lady Vivien Eveleigh."

"How do you know that?" Winston demanded.

Rosa's heart dropped into her stomach. Finally, she answered weakly, "Because he was in jail."

"You're right, Miss Reed," Chief Inspector Fredricks said. "He was one month into a two-month sentence in Stanfield Prison for harassing Miss Jane Stimpson."

CHAPTER 15

*B*asil and Ginger got up to see both Chief Inspector Fredericks and Winston to the door while Rosa and Miguel remained seated on the settee next to the fire. Rosa felt stunned, and neither of them said a word for a full minute.

"He told me he was at home ill that night," Rosa finally muttered.

"I guess that's more palatable than telling you he was in jail on charges of harassment."

"I keep thinking about Vivien's final moments." Rosa closed her eyes and took a deep breath. "I don't want to, but those thoughts keep forcing their way in."

Miguel kissed the top of her head.

"The killer was a thief, all right," Rosa continued,

her voice low and thick with emotion. "Vivien would have been there when I finished at the police training school, and I would have been at her graduation from university. There would have been laughter, tears. I was robbed too." Rosa put her head on Miguel's shoulder and drew a long, shaky breath.

"We're not done yet," Miguel said.

"I know, but I'm so tired."

"I'm here. If you run out of steam, I have enough for both of us. We are going to find the killer."

"I'm so glad you came." Rosa reached for his hand and squeezed it.

"Time to take another look at Gerald Withers," Miguel said. "We've already debunked his alibi. Let's go dig a little deeper. Joan Freeman is also still a possibility. She had motive, after all. She obviously had feelings for Clive Blackmore and was jealous of his obsession with Vivien. Maybe one night, she had enough and broke into Kenway House, strangled Vivien, and then made it look like a robbery. She certainly looks strong enough to do it. She's also left-handed."

"Yes, but after all these years, it's going to be very difficult to go and chase all that down."

"I'm up for it, if need be."

Rosa nodded and smiled. Just then, Ginger came back into the room.

"Can I speak to you in private, Rosa?"

"Sure, I can leave . . ." Miguel got up.

"No, no. You stay here in front of the fire. Rosa, I'll see you in the usual spot."

They met in Rosa's room, with Rosa sitting on her bed and Ginger sitting on the chair in front of the vanity facing the bed. When Rosa was growing up, they had had many talks in exactly the same manner. Just like the library was the father and daughter spot, this was the mother and daughter spot. In fact, when Ginger had first told Rosa of the plans to send her to California when Rosa was a young teenager, it was with Rosa sitting cross-legged on this very bed and Ginger sitting on that very chair. That conversation had changed Rosa's life.

Feeling like she was thirteen again, she moved her pillows out of the way, leaned back against the headboard, and sat with her legs crossed and tucked close. Whatever her mother wanted to talk about, Rosa had the feeling it might be important. Either that or she was about to be scolded for something.

"It sounded like your drive out in the country the other day was quite adventurous." Ginger crossed her legs and folded her hands in her lap.

Uh-oh. Rosa was in trouble.

Her mother continued, "You were out very late, and the next morning the film developer and fixer containers had less fluid in them. I haven't been in there for a week, but the smell of chemicals was still evident the next morning. I assumed you'd taken some wonderful photos of the countryside."

Now Rosa really felt like a schoolgirl again. She should have known *not* to attempt to fool her mother. She tried hard to keep her face impassive, but Ginger's penetrating gaze was as formidable as ever.

Rosa started to say something but thought better of it.

"You showed us those delightful pictures of you and Miguel from your sightseeing adventures here in London, but oddly enough, nothing from your drive in the country. It was a wonderful day if I recall. I should like to see them sometime."

"Mum, I—"

"I didn't even ask you where you went. First, I thought perhaps Harlow, but now I am guessing you went further to the east?" Ginger cocked her head and raised her eyebrows.

"Guilty as charged," Rosa said. She held out her

hands with her wrists together, as if waiting to be handcuffed.

"Don't be silly," Ginger said. "I don't own a pair of handcuffs anymore." She leaned forward and glanced at the door. "I don't plan on telling your father anything, though I'm pretty sure he has a set somewhere."

"I'm sorry." It was all Rosa could think to say.

"No harm done, I suppose. It's good the man is in jail now, for the sake of the other two women he was following." Ginger absentmindedly picked a piece of lint off her blouse. "Besides, I'd be acting like a hypocrite if I claimed not to have done similar 'investigations' in my past."

Rosa tried very hard not to smirk by suddenly becoming fascinated with a spot on the ceiling.

"Breaking into people's homes should not become a habit, though," Ginger added sternly.

"No, of course not."

"I remain concerned about you, Rosa. Are you going to continue investigating?"

Rosa hesitated before answering. "We have one or two more stones to turn over."

"Such as?"

Rosa had already told her about Joan Freeman. Still, as she talked about Gerald Withers and how

Miguel had discovered that his alibi was false, Ginger's eyebrows knit together.

"What's the matter?" Rosa asked.

"You and Miguel form a very sharp investigative team, but I fear that your combined talents have led you down the wrong path in this case as well."

Rosa's mouth dropped open. "What?"

Ginger worked her lips. "You must abandon your investigation of Gerald Withers at once."

Shocked, Rosa asked, "How do you even know Gerald Withers?"

"I don't really know him well, but—"

"Then how can you be so sure he is not guilty? I've already told you that his alibi is a lie!"

"Yes, it is."

Rosa just stared at her mother.

"You have to trust me, Rosa." Ginger's mouth set in a hard line.

"You have to give me something, Mum. This isn't just any case; this is *Vivien*."

Ginger hesitated and then raised her hand in the air. "All right, all right. You do deserve to know something." She huffed and smoothed the wrinkles from her pencil skirt while Rosa waited. "What I am about to tell you must *never* leave this room. Do you understand?" Ginger looked directly into Rosa's eyes.

"Of course."

"Not even Miguel."

Rosa blinked. That would be hard, but she would do it. "All right, not even Miguel."

"Do the names Donald Maclean and Guy Burgess mean anything to you?"

Rosa thought for a moment. "Yes, I seem to recall something about men spying for the Soviet Union or something. It was in the press. That was a while ago."

"1951. Right around the same time that Vivien was killed."

"I guess so," Rosa said, dragging the words out. What could spies for Russia possibly have to do with Vivien's case?

"Donald Maclean and Guy Burgess were long-time members of British intelligence and worked with the Foreign Office. They were both very active in the war and later worked under the guise of being diplomats in America and other places. Early in 1951, they suddenly defected to Russia, leaving everyone at the Foreign Office bewildered. It turned out later that they were part of a spy ring called the *Cambridge Five*. That much is public knowledge."

"Oh yes, I remember that now." Rosa nodded and waited for her mother to continue.

"What most people don't know is that there was a secret commission set up here in London to investigate just how far the double agents' lies had gone and who was involved in forming the Cambridge Five." She paused, looking at Rosa, who nodded.

"Okay."

Her mother continued. "Anyone who had collaborated with any members of the Cambridge Five during the war and who knew them well was called in for initial consultation. The first week of those proceedings took place in the same week that Vivien died."

"Wait." Rosa shook her head. "Are you saying Gerald Withers worked for British intelligence during the war?"

"I am not saying anything." Ginger straightened and again fussed with her blouse.

Understanding dawned on Rosa. "Because you're not allowed to say it."

As Ginger and Rosa's eyes met, Rosa took a deep breath and exhaled slowly. Her mind whirled. Of course! Gerald was old enough to have served in the war. Maybe he had been assigned to some special post, like in covert operations. He was a capable person with a sharp mind and leadership qualities.

"Okay, so, I understand that this must be kept secret," Rosa said slowly. "What I don't understand, in fact, what I am perplexed by . . . is how *you* know all of this. You weren't at these proceedings, were you? You were supposed to be travelling abroad!"

"We were, we were. You saw us off at the train station, remember?"

"Well then, how do you know all of this about Gerald Withers?"

It was the first time in her life Rosa had ever seen such a mixed storm of emotion on her mother's face. Rosa read love, hesitation, resolve, and regret all at the same moment.

"Mum?" Rosa's eyes widened with concern.

Ginger just shook her head. "Please don't ask me to explain."

There was a part of her mother's life that had remained shrouded in mystery. As a child, Rosa had been in awe of how capable her mother was in ways that most women, even most men, were not. She seemed good at *so many* things, from understanding the inner workings of an engine to physical self-defense, picking locks, and reading people's facial expressions. She was an excellent photographer and could speak several languages. When she faked a foreign accent, you would have thought she was someone else. Like Rosa, she was a crack shot and owned a revolver. She remained unflappable, even when danger presented itself. And when it came to solving puzzles, her ability baffled everyone, including Rosa's father, who was brilliant in his own right.

Of course, these were all things that had helped make her such an effective detective.

As Rosa honed her skills, she realized more and more that her mother *must* have undertaken some kind of special training at some point in her life. When Rosa questioned her about it, her mother had shrugged it all off with some vague comment or another until Rosa gave up. Even Rosa's father had once admitted to Rosa that he didn't know everything there was to know about his wife.

Rosa had long ago guessed that the secrets stemmed from something in the First World War. Her mother rarely ever mentioned that period, but Rosa knew her first husband, Lord Daniel Gold, had died as a soldier.

As a girl in her twenties, Ginger had worked as a telephone operator in France. Rosa wondered if her mother had served as a spy for British intelligence.

Perhaps her mother and father had taken part in similar matters throughout World War Two; it would explain why they had sent their daughter to America for the duration. It was well known that British operatives in both conflicts had to swear a lifelong oath of secrecy.

As Rosa watched her mother silently struggle through her emotions, she suddenly realized, once again, how deeply she loved her mother and that her respect for her was incalculable.

"I trust you," was all she could say before walking over to her mother and hugging her tightly.

CHAPTER 16

*R*osa and Miguel strolled hand in hand through Hyde Park, blending in with the dark wool jackets of the other pedestrians, and avoiding bicycles with hurried riders racing in both directions. The weather had turned from a cold, dreary morning to a pleasant afternoon, and they had spontaneously taken a long walk.

"It's not up to California standards, but the sun feels nice," Rosa said. She closed her eyes and turned her face to greet the rays shining through the bare branches of a common lime tree towering above the pathway.

"I phoned the department last night, just to check in, like," Miguel said. "They want me back by the end of the month."

"That's still over two weeks away," Rosa returned. "They've been very understanding."

"I agree. But I want you to know that if it takes longer than that, I'm staying right here. I want to see this thing through."

Rosa pulled their clasped hands to her lips and kissed Miguel's knuckle. "I appreciate that you are willing to stay, Miguel, but I don't want you to put your position in jeopardy. You're too important there. Besides that . . ." She took a deep breath. "I'm thinking we're at a dead end."

"What do you mean? We still have to check out Gerald Withers—"

"We have to take him off the suspect list."

"What? Why?"

"I'm afraid I can't tell you."

"The talk with your mother?"

"That's right. I'm sorry, but she made me promise secrecy. All I can say is that Gerald Withers *did* lie about going to Scotland, but he had nothing to do with Vivien's murder, and . . . well, his activities can't be divulged."

"Top secret! The security of the nation is at stake." Miguel laughed at his joke, but stopped when he saw the serious look on Rosa's face.

"Oh, golly. Okay, I won't ask. And, of course, we trust your mother."

"Yes, we do."

"Well then, there's Joan Freeman," Miguel offered.

Rosa sighed. "Checking her alibi will be next to impossible."

"True, but she must have some other friends, maybe a spurned lover. She has a past we can dig into. Somebody has to know something."

Rosa nodded even though she felt her enthusiasm waning. "We should still set some kind of time limit on this, though."

WHEN THEY GOT BACK to Hartigan House, they found Basil sitting in the sitting room reading a newspaper, with his leather-slippered feet up on an ottoman.

"Anything exciting happening in London today?" Miguel asked as he and Rosa stepped inside.

Basil peered over the top of *The London Weekly*. "A man was shot on the street in Croydon three days ago. The killer was apprehended almost straightaway. There was another death in West Kilburn. A woman jumped from her window." He sucked on the pipe in his mouth. "Nasty goings-on in our city."

As far back as Rosa could remember, her father had sat in that same chair smoking a pipe and scouring the dailies for details of murder cases. Even now, long after retirement, he liked to keep his finger on the pulse of the criminal activities in the city, particularly murder cases. Rosa's mother, on the other hand, had no interest in such things anymore. Her nose could be found either in fashion magazines or in the social columns of the newspapers.

Collins appeared and handed a white envelope to Rosa. "A letter for you, miss."

Rosa stared at the envelope. The return address read, Notting Hill Carmelite Monastery, 87 St Charles Square, London. "That's odd." She couldn't imagine who would write to her from a monastery or why. Miguel and Basil chatted about the London crime rate as she ripped open the envelope. Inside was a handwritten letter.

Dear Miss Reed,

I hope you are well and enjoying the blessings of all this good weather we seem to have here in our lovely city.

My name is Sister Dorothy Montgomery, and I obtained your address from my nephew Constable Cyril Halstead with whom I've learned you are acquainted. Cyril mentioned that you had recently arrived in London and that you were a good friend of Lady Vivien Eveleigh before she died and are connected to the Eveleigh family.

A spinster who I know because of her association with the monastery, a Miss Francine Deane, has recently died. The police can't determine if it was suicide or an accident, though I'm dearly hoping for the latter. She met her maker after a fall from a fourth-storey window. My heart is broken.

Because Francine has no living relatives, she had some time ago named me the executor of her estate, as small as it is. She had been having problems remembering things last year and had entrusted me with her papers. Recently, I came across something that puzzled me. Now that she has passed away, I can't seem to stop thinking about it. It might not be significant, and I hate to bother you, but I wonder if you wouldn't mind calling at the monastery sometime while you are here.

If so, please contact me through the monastery, and we can arrange a suitable time.

May His peace be upon you and yours,

Sister Dorothy Montgomery

"Is everything all right?"

Rosa came back to attention at the sound of Miguel's voice. He and her father were looking at her with interest and concern.

"I think so," she said. "Dad, can I please see that story about the woman who fell from the window?"

EARLY THE FOLLOWING DAY, Rosa and Miguel took a short ride on the underground to Ladbroke Grove station near St Charles Square. Notting Hill Carmelite Monastery was a massive two-story brick complex surrounded by a twenty-two-foot stone wall and flanked by expansive gardens. They approached the double-wide, ten-foot-high wooden gate, and Rosa rang a bell to announce their arrival.

Miguel pointed to a brass plaque embedded in the wall that read "Established 1878—Dedicated to the vision of being a centre of contemplative prayer in the heart of the city."

"I could probably use more of that," Miguel remarked.

"Contemplative prayer?"

"Yes, I was raised Catholic. I even thought of becoming a monk at one time." He crossed himself as he looked up at a small crucifix embedded in the wall.

Rosa raised her eyebrows in surprise. "Really? When?"

"When I was eleven. Although, by the time I hit

twelve, I discovered the guitar and because of that, girls." He flashed Rosa a brilliant grin.

"Two very onerous temptations," Rosa returned with a smile.

The gate creaked as it slowly swung open, and they were greeted by a nun in her mid-fifties with bright, sparkling, blue eyes and wire-framed spectacles. She wore a black habit that fell to her feet, but Rosa could just make out the toes of some very worn black-leather shoes.

"Good morning," Rosa began. "I'm Miss Rosa Reed, and this is my friend, Detective Miguel Belmonte. Sister Dorothy Montgomery has requested to see me."

The nun smiled shyly, bowed slightly, and without saying a word, gestured for them to come in. Down a wide stone walkway, they followed her, past the main building flanked on both sides by large gardens and several smaller buildings. The gardens featured a stand of mature deciduous trees and hedges. Rosa could see several nuns engaged in hoeing a vegetable patch, chopping wood, and painting what looked to be a newly built wooden chair. None spoke a word.

The nun gestured to a one-level brick building

with Guest Reception written on a sign on the wooden door.

Inside was a sparsely furnished but comfortable small reception room with windows looking out on the garden. Besides a large fireplace, several upholstered chairs and sofas circled a woolen, gray throw rug lying on the flagstones in the middle.

The nun motioned for them to take a seat, then disappeared.

Rosa raised a brow and whispered to Miguel, "Are we allowed to speak?"

Miguel shrugged and whispered back. "I wouldn't know. Like I said, I gave up my pursuit of the vocation at twelve."

They didn't have to wait long as a tall, earthy nun entered. Rosa and Miguel stood as she extended her hand, and Rosa noticed garden soil under her fingernails.

"Good day," she said. "I'm Sister Dorothy."

"Thank you for seeing us," Rosa said. "I hope we aren't intruding."

"Not at all. It's our Day of Silence spent working in the gardens. However, Our Lord understands there will be moments when speaking is necessary. Please sit down."

Rosa and Miguel returned to their seats as Sister Dorothy took a seat across from them.

"First, thank you so much for coming to see me. After I sent the letter, I wondered if I am not making too much of this."

"You've piqued my curiosity, and I have to admit, this is my first time in such a place." Rosa smiled. "It's worth the time just to see it."

"Thank you," Sister Dorothy said. With her eyes flashing with interest, she folded her hands on her lap.

"I understand your concern is for a Miss Francine Deane who may have committed suicide," Rosa said.

"Yes. I knew her rather well, and for many years. As I mentioned in the letter, Miss Deane wasn't a woman of great means, but she contributed to our charities, specifically those concerned with helping orphans. She was also often involved in planning fundraisers and did a lot of volunteer work. I often wondered why she hadn't become a nun as she never married and had no family." Sister Dorothy folded her hands on her lap again and shook her head. "I just don't believe she took her own life."

"An accident then?" Rosa asked.

"Francine started having problems remembering

things. Sometimes she would repeat herself. Then, two months ago, she left here to return to her flat. Two hours later, she came back confused. She couldn't find her way! I had to take her home."

"Was Miss Deane the depressive type?" Miguel asked.

"On the contrary. She was a very cheerful person and always had a certain zest for life. We had just spoken the day before she died, and she was quite excited about an event coming up at the Royal Merchant Seamen's Orphanage. It was supposed to be held in two weeks. Some children she had become close to were performing in a play. Her mind might have been diminishing, but her enthusiasm for life was still very much intact." Sister Dorothy wrung her hands together. "I cannot imagine her throwing herself from her window, but there you have it."

Rosa and Miguel digested that information.

"But let me show you what I found," the nun said brightly, reaching down and opening the brown-leather satchel strapped over her shoulder. "As I mentioned in the letter, she had made me responsible for her estate because she knew her memory was failing. She has, or rather had, a bank account at the London Central Bank. A while ago, I went through her belongings and found this ledger." She handed a small notebook to Rosa. "It contains private financial records that I assume are related to her income and expenses. A simple balance record if you will."

Rosa was puzzled, but with Miguel looking on, she leafed through the pages. The notations went back over thirty years, and some pages were very faded. Handwritten records of monthly expenses such as rent, food, clothes, and charity donations were scribbled in the margins.

Starting March 1923, there was only one figure written in the income column each month. It represented a modest income of £4 a month in 1923 and then gradually went up a small amount every three months until it reached £28 per month. It was enough for a single person to live comfortably if one was frugal enough. The last entry was about a month earlier.

"Did Miss Deane ever mention how she made her living?" Miguel asked.

"No, she never mentioned it to anyone. We all assumed she had a trust fund or something, but it wasn't any of our business, so we didn't ask. But now that she's gone, I wonder."

Rosa continued to leaf through the pages. "I am

not sure what this has to do with our—" She stopped suddenly and stared at the entries for September 1947.

"It's probably nothing," Sister Dorothy said when she noticed Rosa had stopped turning the pages. "Certainly nothing to bother an important lord about, but I thought because you are a friend of the family, you might have some insight." She paused, then added, "I don't want to poke my head into someone else's business . . ."

"Thank you for this," Rosa said, staring at the page. "You were right to contact me."

As Miguel leaned over to look at the ledger, Rosa blinked and stared at the page again. Though it was not as neatly written as the rest of the notations, it was clearly Francine Deane's handwriting that scrawled out Winston Eveleigh's name at the top of the page.

$\mathcal{B}$ack in the "case room" at Hartigan House, Rosa and Miguel scoured through the notebook for any other clues but came up empty. No names were attached to the entries directly, and there was no mention from where the mysterious monthly income was coming.

Rosa closed the book with a sigh. "The whole thing is so strange. There's no obvious connection between this woman and the Eveleigh family."

"Maybe we should ask Winston if the name Francine Deane rings any bells," Miguel said. "He's the only surviving Eveleigh. When did his parents die, again?"

"If I remember correctly, it was July 1948" Rosa

said. "Two months before Winston Eveleigh's name was most likely written at the top of that page."

Rosa pressed a finger to her lips. "Perhaps we could ask him, but if anything about this compromises Winston, it would be easy for him just to deny any knowledge of it. And it could be something as innocent as Miss Deane simply hearing about Winston somewhere and subconsciously doodling his name in the ledger, flicking it open to a random page. Sister Dorothy was concerned about Miss Deane's state of mind."

"That's true," Miguel said absentmindedly. He walked to the picture board and pointed. "What's that?"

On the right bottom corner of the board, partially hidden by notes, was a photograph of a crumpled page that had been spread out, like the pages from the notebook they'd just looked through.

"That's the paper that was found in Vivien's pocket," Rosa said. She unpinned the photograph from the board, returned to the notebook on the table, and flipped through its pages again.

"Here!" She glanced up at Miguel as she pointed to the sheet of paper in front of her. "The numbers on the crumpled page are in Vivien's handwriting, and they look to be hastily written ledger entries of outgoing monthly expenses. However, nothing that corresponded to these numbers was found in Vivien's ledgers. See, there are fourteen numbers listed." Rosa held up the photograph.

"But now, look." Rosa flipped through the ledger and showed Miguel the last fourteen months leading up to Vivien's death. The income numbers from Francine Deane's ledger matched exactly and sequentially with the numbers on the piece of paper found on Vivien's body.

"Somebody was making a monthly payment to Francine," Miguel observed.

"Yes, every three months, the amount went up just a bit," Rosa returned. "Perhaps to adjust for rising living costs. The question is, why? And how were Vivien and Winston involved? This proves a connection between Vivien and Miss Deane, but does it have anything to do with Vivien's demise?" It was a mystery, but Rosa couldn't see how one thing was connected with the other.

Miguel whistled. "At least we now have some pieces. We just have to put the puzzle together."

"SPEAKING OF PUTTING PIECES TOGETHER," Rosa said, "we have to decide how to spend our afternoon. My parents want to meet for dinner tonight at my dad's favorite restaurant in Kensington, so we have a few hours. I want to go to Kenway House and sort through Vivien's things to get them ready for the charities. I'm ready to face it now."

Miguel looked at her. "Do you need me there?"

Rosa thought for a moment, then shook her head. "I think I'd rather be alone for this, and it would be a bore for you."

"Winston said he wouldn't be there, so I'd lose my usual heartwarming conversations with him. Shame." Miguel grinned crookedly, one dimple to tease her. "And you know how much I love those."

"Uh-huh." Rosa nodded doubtfully and then cocked her head, "I feel you have something else you want to do."

"I thought I'd go to that pub you mentioned. The Baron's . . . something."

"The Baron's Goose?"

"That's it. The place where Winston claimed to be on the night of the murder."

Rosa scrunched her brows. "But why? That came to a dead end a long time ago. Winston's alibi is solid."

"I know, I know. But it doesn't hurt to snoop

around. That's what detectives do, as you know. Force of habit."

"Yes, I heard that," Rosa said, rolling her eyes. "Very well, I'll show you a map and how to get there by underground. Do you think you can navigate there and back on your own?"

"Piece of cake," Miguel said. "Which is what I hope they serve at that pub, by the way."

Rosa laughed, knowing Miguel was sure to be disappointed. "You'd better set your sights on meat pie."

BEING BACK at Kenway House again shot an odd feeling through Rosa. As Winston had explained, the second floor of the Victorian manor had been updated. Rosa scanned the room; the only piece of Vivien's furniture remaining was her favorite leather-upholstered reading chair. The carpeting, wallpaper, and paint throughout the rest of the level had all been changed. Obviously, Winston had hired professional interior decorators because everything was tastefully appointed and color-matched.

Rosa had been greeted at the front door by Winston's dour-looking butler, Stevens, who informed her that Winston was not in at the moment, but he had been instructed to give Rosa access to the second floor, and all the time she needed to go through Vivien's things. The staff had the day off, so Stevens was the only one there at the moment, although he, too, would be leaving soon for the day.

As Rosa was led down the familiar hallway and past the large room that had served as Vivien's drawing room, many memories swirled in her mind. How many hours had they spent in that room? Images of herself and Vivien sitting on a sofa drinking tea and sharing stories about their studies flew through her mind's eye. They'd mused about the future. Vivien planned to be a solicitor, and Rosa wanted to be a detective. They had laughed a lot. Sometimes they'd played cards, especially an Italian game they both loved called *Machiavelli*, like rummy, minus the gambling component. Vivien had hosted wonderful get-togethers in that room. But, to Rosa's memory, Winston had not been present at any of them, a fact which now struck her as odd despite him being five years her senior.

Rosa was shown to a nicely renovated study, which had formerly served as a guest bedroom.

Stevens gestured for Rosa to enter the room. "Lady Vivien's things are stored in boxes in the storage cupboard. Lord Eveleigh has instructed me to leave you to look through them." With that, he bowed and walked away.

The closet had once been an extended sitting room and was now used for storage. Winston had arranged for all of Vivien's leftover items to be stored here, awaiting sorting and distribution to appropriate charities. Beside several cardboard boxes, there was also a set of golf clubs, two tennis racquets, and white athletic shoes. Rosa remembered Vivien telling her that she had no time for athletics once she had entered university.

Rosa started with the nearest box and opened it. The first item she pulled out was a worn, stuffed teddy bear.

"Cecil!" Rosa said as she hugged the bear.

It had been Vivien's favorite stuffed toy since she was a child. Rosa made a spontaneous decision. "Cecil, you're going to emigrate to America and meet a very mischievous cat." She held the bear out at arm's length. "Perhaps you'll be a calming influence on him."

Cecil would make an excellent companion and a cherished memory of Vivien and would have an honored place on Rosa's bedroom bureau. The thought of that made Rosa smile. She pulled more stuffed animals out of the box, a half-dozen pairs of shoes, some knickknacks and small collectibles. She wrote each item on her notepad and placed them on the floor. After emptying the box, she carefully placed the items back in, now having a record of what was inside.

She moved the box next to the door and then repeated the whole process with several other boxes. A larger, heavier box was loaded with books and photo albums. Opening the first photo album, Rosa scanned the many pictures of Vivien, mainly from the age of thirteen and older. There were several pictures of Rosa and Vivien together. One had them posing in front of a dress display at Selfridges. Rosa laughed as she remembered some of the absurd outfits they had tried on that day.

Like sisters, Rosa thought as tears rolled down her cheeks.

Her next thought was much darker. She was Vivien's best friend, and despite being a police constable, she couldn't solve this most important case. The cruel irony made Rosa wince. After letting the tears flow for a few moments, she dried her eyes and continued to look through the box. At the very bottom, she found a partial set of hardcover encyclo-pedias. Pulling the last one out of the box, Rosa accidentally dropped the book, and it fell to the floor open. Stuck inside the pages was a thin leather-bound notebook with "Vivien Eveleigh" written on the front.

A journal? How odd to find it hidden away in the middle of an encyclopedia. Rosa paused for a moment with her hand resting on the cover before opening it.

The journal was filled with private musings, a few poems, and even some sketches. Rosa felt uncomfortable scrolling through it—she was spying on someone's inner thoughts—however, it was clear that Vivien had purposely hidden this book, and the police had never discovered it. Had she done it simply out of the wish for privacy?

On a page dated Feb 15, 1951, just one month before Vivien's death, Winston's name caught Rosa's eye.

CHAPTER 18

Today Winston threatened me again. He told me he would throw me out without a penny if I don't do everything he says precisely the way he says it. That he is the firstborn and has precedence to any claims of family assets as set out in our parents' will, makes me believe he'll do it one day. I hope to marry well, yet Winston undermines my prospects there by telling vicious lies that soil my reputation.

Today, he uttered his usual threat casually and without emotion. He takes pleasure in causing me to feel shame and teases me relentlessly about my weight when I was younger, often in front of my friends. He is charming and engaging in public, but in private, one must walk on eggshells around him. This is why I must succeed on my own, and I'll do it by building my career as a solicitor. I can't wait for that day to see the smug grin wiped off his face when I walk out of the front door, immune to his threats.

A lump rose in Rosa's throat as she read Vivien's words. She flipped over a few pages until she came to an entry dated March 2, 1951. Two weeks before her death. It was the last entry in the journal.

Yesterday, I discovered something that will change everything! My mind is reeling at the ramifications. Winston was out for the day, and I'd thought it would be an excellent time to go into his quarters and look for our estate financial and legal records. He's taken care of our family's legal and financial matters since our parents died. But something made me believe he wasn't telling me everything.

I thoroughly searched his office desk and found a hidden drawer. Inside was a key. After fiddling around with the key, I finally found that it opened the filing cabinets. I quickly unlocked everything and opened the first drawer.

At first, everything seemed as it should be, and I almost missed it. But in the last file box, at the back, was a single folder with no markings or designation of any kind. Inside I found a separate journal containing transaction records going back several years. The first pages were in our father's handwriting, with notations showing amounts being paid monthly to someone named Francine Deane. The amounts increased incrementally over the years, and I wondered if Father had been fostering a secret life. Perhaps a long-time mistress in some flat in London somewhere? My mind refused to imagine this. As I read on, I discovered that the handwriting changed after our parents' deaths.

Winston had taken over the payments.

This puzzled me deeply until I looked through the file again. In a white envelope, faded with time and folded into four parts, was a birth certificate. On November 3, 1921, Francine Deane gave birth to a baby boy at St Jude's Convent in North London. Sister Mary Anderson, likely a midwife, had signed the certificate. The boy was christened Winston Deane.

November 3 is Winston's birthday.

The pieces fell together quickly in my mind. A forbidden love affair between my father and this mystery woman. An unplanned pregnancy. Secrets insured by a modest monthly stipend.

So why didn't they just pay Francine Deane to raise the child on her own? I can only guess. Perhaps Father wanted to ensure a male heir, or perhaps Francine

Deane was unwell. When our parents died, Francine Deane must have approached Winston with the whole story. Possibly given him the birth certificate as proof. Whatever it was, he was convinced enough to continue with the payments.

Those are details that may well be forever lost in time, but if my theory is correct, one thing is certain; Winston is illegitimate and wouldn't have the legal right to the family fortune. He might not even be a lord! Perhaps that's why his threats seem to get more pronounced as time goes on. Perhaps Francine Deane wants more money.

I was going to fetch my camera to take pictures of the transaction records and the birth certificate, but I suddenly heard Winston's voice talking to our butler on the ground floor. I quickly jotted down a few of the financial entries, locked everything up, and hurried out of the room. Perhaps I should have taken the file, but I was afraid that Winston would sense my trespass. If I'm going to confront him on this, I want the power of choosing the moment myself.

I plan to search for Francine Deane tomorrow. If I find she is still alive and my theory proves true, I will confront Winston. I have no idea how he'll react, but it must be done.

After over five years in the grave, Vivien had finally broken her silence.

Rosa leaned back in the chair with one hand on her mouth and her mind spinning. Her hand holding the journal fell loosely to her side, letting go of the notebook. It fell to the floor just as a familiar voice came from the open door.

CHAPTER 19

"Oh, you're here."

Rosa sprang to her feet at Winston's voice.

"Are you all right?" Winston said with a smirk. "You look like you've seen a ghost!"

Rosa watched his gaze fall to the notebook lying open on the floor, and the harsh realization that she was alone with a killer suddenly tightened her throat.

"No . . . not a ghost exactly," she stammered, trying to keep her voice even while she reached down to pick up the journal. "But it is a queer feeling going through all of her things." She glanced around the room, trying her best to look wistful and melancholy. "I . . . I think I've finished for today. It's surprising how emotional her loss has left me after all these years."

She walked over to a small desk, keeping her back to Winston as she slipped the notebook into her handbag. "If you don't mind," she said, "I'll come back tomorrow and finish up." When she turned to face him, his eyes were locked on her, his expression grim.

"Of course, I understand." He was smiling, but the look of suspicion in his eyes was sharp. "Please feel free to come again tomorrow."

Rosa smiled faintly, nodded, and quickly ducked past him in the door as he stepped out of her way.

"Belmonte isn't here with you?"

"Uh, no."

"Oh, I almost forgot," Winston said as Rosa started down the corridor. "I have something of Vivien's down in my place that I think you should have as a keepsake. Let's stop there before you go."

"I really think I—"

"No, no, I insist. I probably won't be here tomorrow when you return, and I don't want to forget." This time his smile seemed more genuine.

"It must be something important," Rosa said with forced cheer.

"Yes, it is, and small too. You will have no

problem putting it in your luggage when you return to California. I know she would have wanted you to have it. You'll be surprised." He walked past her in the hall and gestured for her to follow.

Rosa made a split-second decision to do as he asked, keeping her distance as much as she could. If she behaved uncharacteristically, she would stir his suspicions and make her escape more difficult.

They walked into his living room area, which was virtually unchanged from when Rosa had been there last, over a year before. Shortly after Vivien's death, Winston had replaced the furniture and had hired a designer to change the color scheme and decor. Since then, Rosa had been there many times. After her time away in California, being there now felt as if she were walking into a dream, familiar and yet surreal.

Winston smiled and gestured for her to sit on the leather sofa. "Please."

"I'd rather not." Rosa stood in the middle of the living room clutching her handbag. "My parents are expecting me—"

A dark look passed through his eyes. "Suit yourself."

Winston opened a drawer in the sideboard and produced a small blue ornamental box no bigger than his palm. He handed it to her. "I believe she would want you to have this."

Inside was a beautifully engraved silver, heart-shaped locket necklace. Inside the locket was a small photograph of Vivien. It looked like the picture had been taken shortly before her death. Rosa remembered she had not long before changed her hairstyle to a shorter, wavier bouffant. Looking at it now, Rosa realized that the new style made her look like little-known Italian actress Sophia Loren, who Rosa had seen in the film *The Gold of Naples*.

At that moment, the lack of resemblance between Winston and Vivien hit her. One would never guess they were siblings.

"It's beautiful," she said sincerely. "Thank you."

It was a stunning locket, and Rosa planned to wear it with the fondest memories. Emotion welled up again as Rosa looked at the image of her dear friend smiling in the photograph.

"I meant to give it to you as a gift at our wedding," Winston said, "But, of course . . ." He let the sentence go unfinished.

"I'm sor—"

Winston stepped to her side. "Let me help you put it on."

"I—"

"At least let me see you wearing it. You owe me that much."

To avoid revealing her hand—that she now knew him to be the villain she'd feared he was, Rosa relented, though she kept her wits on high alert, ready to spring into action, if she had to. Slowly, she turned her back to him and held up the hair on the nape of her neck. Winston reached around her from behind, the chain of the necklace between his fingers. Rosa shivered at how close he stood—not like a lady enticed by a man, overcome with feelings of romance, but by apprehension. Winston had strangled Vivien to death, and here he was with his fingers so close to her throat.

"There," he said, and Rosa twirled away out of reach. Her fingers trembled as they played with the locket at her neck.

"Thank you. This means a lot. Now I must—"

As Rosa attempted to pass, Winston stepped in front of the open doorway and grabbed her wrist. *With his left hand.*

"I think I would like to take a look at that note-book you were reading."

"Let me go, Winston."

"It was some sort of diary, wasn't it? Did my sister have secrets I should know about?"

"Aren't you the one with secrets?" Rosa said.

"What on earth are you . . .?"

"Francine Deane didn't throw herself out of a window, did she?"

Winston's expression instantly went cold.

Rosa jerked her arm, but Winston refused to release his grip. His mouth turned into a hard line. Then, through clenched teeth, he snarled. "What . . . is . . . in . . . that . . . book?"

Rosa instinctively stepped backward, causing Winston to be slightly off his balance. Shifting her handbag over her shoulder, she stepped sideways, moving her weight to her right foot, and with her left, directed a sharp kick to the side of Winston's right knee. It was a blow that could break a leg, but because she caught him on the inside of the knee, it only buckled sideways, causing him to fall.

"Ow!" he cried out but still stubbornly held on to her wrist with his left hand.

Shifting her weight now to her other foot, she twisted hard and, with an angry shout, brought down her free hand hard on his left forearm.

Winston gasped in pain and let go of her.

She then ran for the door of his flat with her handbag flying along at her side.

"Come back here, you witch!"

Rosa heard his footsteps on the wooden floor and, to her dismay, realized that he would give chase. Glad she was wearing low-heeled shoes, she ran through the open doorway of his living area, down the corridor, and toward the main stairway. He was only a few steps behind her. Would she make it down the stairs at top speed without falling?

As Rosa ran through the doorway that opened to the top landing of the stairs, she sensed a movement to her immediate right but kept running for the head of the stairs. She stopped when she heard a grunt and the thudding sound of Winston's body crashing to the floor.

She turned just in time to see Miguel standing over Winston, who was gasping for breath from having the wind knocked out of him when he landed hard on his back.

"We call that being clothes-lined," Miguel said. "I would stay down there if I were you, *old chap.*"

CHAPTER 20

*R*osa's emotional turmoil was hard to express. Her relief that Vivien's case was finally solved was immense but overshadowed by the fact that Winston, Vivien's brother and someone Rosa had once believed she loved and had almost married, was a murderer.

Oh, the life of misery she would be living right now if her father hadn't given her that last-minute prompting to flee.

It wasn't like her parents hadn't expressed their doubts about a union with Winston, but they hadn't had anything solid to bring against him. On the contrary, to the world, he seemed like a perfect catch: titled, monied, sophisticated, and, at least in appearance, a gentleman.

She glanced at Miguel, glad that he had entered back into her life. They were spending the day wandering down Charing Cross Road, drinking coffee in coffee shops, and window shopping. They'd just finished browsing the aisles of Foyles, a popular bookstore on the ground level of a four-story brick building with residential flats above it. After purchasing a copy of the latest Patricia Wentworth book, she gripped Miguel's hand and squeezed.

He responded by wrapping an arm around her, the comfort he'd offered many times since Winston's arrest three days previously.

Miguel had arrived at Kenway House in the nick of time, having been tipped off by his visit to the Baron's Goose. Six years before, the owner had assured the police that Winston had been there the whole night and even showed the constables the room where Winston stayed. Moreover, Winston had conveniently left behind his wallet, which validated the owner's story.

In the meantime, the owner, Felix Browning, had passed away, and his wife now ran the tavern. She hadn't been questioned by the police when Vivien had died, and with Miguel, she was ready to talk. Mrs. Browning had lived under the thumb of her husband, with no love lost.

"He's not about to shut me up now," she'd said and confessed that Mr. Browning had been indebted to Lord Eveleigh. "He lied to the police about Winston's whereabouts. I saw Lord Eveleigh leave the pub and return about two hours later."

And yes, she would testify because she was no fan of men, gentlemen or otherwise, who mistreated ladies like her.

After that conversation, Miguel had gone straight to Kenway house. Knowing Rosa was there and seeing what he assumed was Winston's car in the driveway made his blood race with a sense of urgency. When no one responded to his knock at the door, he just walked in.

So far, Winston hadn't admitted to anything, which wasn't surprising. Still, the prosecution would have no problem proposing a scenario in which Winston staged the robbery, including the climb up the trellis, breaking his own window, and ransacking the place.

And the mysterious missing golden cufflink? It had likely fallen off one day while Winston was out and about. It could have been missing for years. But when he realized the police were using it to incriminate Briggs, he decided to let them continue with that theory as long as it pointed suspicion away from him.

The spinster, Miss Francine Deane, was Winston's biological mother, a fact Winston was reluctant to have come to light, primarily since it would've meant that he would lose his title, and in his opinion, irreparably mar his reputation. He denied having anything to do with Miss Deane's untimely demise, though he couldn't account for his whereabouts at her time of death.

It didn't matter. A man could only hang once.

Rosa and Miguel ended up in Trafalgar Square, blending into a cluster of people wearing wool jackets and felt hats. Red double-decker buses with rounded rooftops and sides covered in adverts for Nescafé and Wrigley's, Gordon's Gin and Bile Beans filled the lanes of the surrounding streets.

"Is there a quieter place we can go?" Miguel asked.

Rosa nodded. "We can head toward the Thames and walk along the Victoria Embankment."

Hand in hand, they reached the slow-moving muddy waters of the River Thames as it flowed east toward the North Sea.

"Which way?" Rosa asked.

Miguel hummed as he gazed in both directions. "I wouldn't mind another glimpse of Big Ben."

Rosa was happy with his choice. She was in the mood for a longer, meandering stroll. "Should we get tired, there are several benches along the way where we can stop and rest." They'd already been walking for some time, and Rosa was ready for the first bench when they reached it.

"London is a spectacular city," Miguel said. "So much history and amazing architecture, it makes the mind spin."

"I didn't think much about it before I went to California," Rosa admitted. "It was the only world I knew. But, now that I've spent time away, I appreciate it more."

Miguel shifted, turning to face Rosa. "Are you still intent on returning to Santa Bonita? With Vivien's case solved and Winston out of your life for good—" He waved at the beautiful view across the river. "This is your home."

Rosa took Miguel's hand. "It *was* my home. I find I'm missing a sunnier, warmer climate, fewer people, and the raw beauty of the desert landscape."

Miguel let out a slow breath; his dark eyes glittered with relief. "You don't know how happy that makes me feel."

Then to her utter amazement, on the rough bricks of the walkway, Miguel slid to one knee.

"I've been carrying this around for a long time, Rosa." He reached into his trouser pocket, opened his wallet to a small buttoned compartment, and withdrew a gold ring graced with a small solitaire. "It was my grandmother's, and not what a girl like you would expect, but—"

Rosa stopped him. "I don't care about the ring, Miguel."

His expression darkened. "You don't want—"

"No, I mean, it's not the ring that's important to me."

"Oh, good, okay, then let me get on with it."

Rosa chuckled. "Please, do."

"Rosa Reed, would you do me the extreme honor of becoming my wife?"

It was the second time he'd asked her. Her mind flashed to the garden behind the Santa Bonita library so many years earlier, another lifetime really, when she had been a teen and he a young soldier. How things had changed.

Life would have been so different for them both had she faced her fears and followed her heart back then. Would the last ten years have been blissfully happy or passionately tortuous? Probably a little of both.

The choices they had made could never be undone, and, Rosa realized, she was glad for the struggle of the years between. They had shaped her into the woman she'd become: strong, resourceful, wise.

"Rosa?"

She smiled at Miguel's worried look and held out her hand, wiggling her ring finger.

"Yes, Miguel Belmonte. I will be your wife."

After a kiss that was much too romantic to be continued in public, they continued their stroll, arm in arm, along the Thames.

NOTE FROM THE AUTHORS

Keen eyed readers might take exception to the timing of the cricket match as relayed in *Murder in London*. The authors acknowledge that in reality, the match wouldn't have occurred during the month this book was set, but agreed that the shared experience depicted between the characters of Basil Reed and Miguel Belmonte was worth taking a small liberty.

We hope you agree!

WHAT'S NEXT?

If you enjoyed reading *Murder in London* please help others enjoy it too.

Recommend it: Help others find the book by recommending it to friends, readers' groups, discussion boards.

Suggest it: to your local library.

Review it: Please tell other readers why you liked this book by reviewing it on Amazon or Goodreads.

** Please don't add spoilers to your review. **

MURDER AT THE FIESTA
A Rosa Reed Mystery #9

Murder's a bash!

When Rosa Reed attends a birthday party at her fiancé's mother's house in the spring of 1957, the Mexican fiesta turns deadly. It's wasn't how Rosa wanted to celebrate her engagement to Detective Miguel Belmonte, nor how she hoped to be introduced to his large family.

Before long, Rosa Reed Investigations is on the case. Can Rosa and Miguel find the murderer before some else dies?

And when will Rosa have time to plan the wedding?

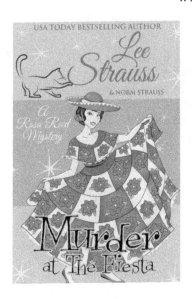

Buy on AMAZON or read for free with Kindle Unlimited!

Rosa & Miguel's Wartime Romance is a BONUS short story exclusively for Lee's newsletter subscribers.

Subscribe Now!

Read on for excerpt.

Don't miss the next Ginger Gold Mystery!

MURDER ON MALLOWAN COURT

Murder's afoot!

As Mrs. Ginger Reed~also known as Lady Gold~waits impatiently for the coming of her baby, new neighbours move onto Mallowan Court. The

Foote family is very much like Ginger's own, if not the mirror opposite: Mr. and Mrs. Foote an unhappy couple; Mr. Rothwell an aging, irate patriarch; Miss Charlotte, whom Scout finds to be a tantalizing, if confusing specimen of young ladyhood; along with a similar collection of staff.

The sudden passing of a Foote family member is determined to be unsuspicious, but something about this strange family doesn't sit right with Ginger.

When the doctor banishes Ginger to her bed to await the coming birth, she has to depend on the information brought to her by her good friend and former sister-in-law, Felicia, the new Lady Davenport-Witt.

Can the two ladies solve the crime before the baby comes?

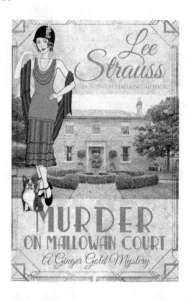

Buy on AMAZON or read for free with Kindle Unlimited!

ROSA & MIGUEL'S WARTIME ROMANCE

PREQUEL - EXCERPT

Rosa Reed first laid eyes on Miguel Belmonte on the fourteenth day of February in 1945. She was a senior attending a high school dance, and he a soldier who played in the band.

She'd been dancing with her date, Tom Hawkins, a short, stalky boy with pink skin and an outbreak of acne, but her gaze continued to latch onto the bronze-skinned singer, with dark crew-cut hair, looking very dapper in a black suit.

In a life-changing moment, their eyes locked. Despite the fact that she stared at the singer over the shoulder of her date, she couldn't help the bolt of electricity that shot through her, and when the singer smiled—and those dimples appeared—heavens, her knees almost gave out!

"Rosa?"

Tom's worried voice brought her back to reality. "Are you okay? You went a little limp there. Do you feel faint? It is mighty hot in here." Tom released Rosa's hand to tug at his tie. "Do you want to get some air?"

Rosa felt a surge of alarm. Invitations to step outside the gymnasium were often euphemisms to get fresh.

In desperation she searched for her best friend Nancy Davidson—her best *American* friend, that was. Vivien Eveleigh claimed the position of *best* friend back in London, and Rosa missed her. Nancy made for a sufficient substitute. A pretty girl with honey-blond hair, Nancy, fortunately, was no longer dancing, and was sitting alone.

"I think I'll visit the ladies, Tom, if you don't mind."

He looked momentarily put out, then shrugged. "Suit yourself." He joined a group of lads—boys—at the punch table, and joined in with their raucous laughter. Rosa didn't want to know what they were joking about, or at whose expense.

Nancy understood Rosa's plight as she wasn't entirely pleased with her fellow either. "If only you and I could dance with each other."

"One can't very well go to a dance without a date, though," Rosa said.

Nancy laughed. "*One* can't."

Rosa rolled her eyes. Even after four years of living in America, her Englishness still manifested when she was distracted.

And tonight's distraction was the attractive lead singer in the band, and shockingly, he seemed to have sought her face out too.

Nancy had seen the exchange and gave Rosa a firm nudge. "No way, José. I know he's cute, but he's from the wrong side of the tracks. Your aunt would have a conniption."

Nancy wasn't wrong about that. Aunt Louisa had very high standards, as one who was lady of Forrester mansion, might.

"I'm only looking!"

Nancy harrumphed. "As long as it stays that way."

Continue reading >>>

Subscribe Now!

On AMAZON

THE ROSA REED MYSTERIES

(1950s cozy historical)

Murder at High Tide

Murder on the Boardwalk

Murder at the Bomb Shelter

Murder on Location

Murder and Rock 'n' Roll

Murder at the Races

Murder at the Dude Ranch

Murder in London

Murder at the Fiesta

GINGER GOLD MYSTERY SERIES (cozy 1920s historical)

Cozy. Charming. Filled with Bright Young Things. This Jazz Age murder mystery will entertain and delight you with its 1920s flair and pizzazz!

LADY GOLD INVESTIGATES (Ginger Gold companion short stories)

HIGGINS & HAWKE MYSTERY SERIES (cozy 1930s historical)

The 1930s meets Rizzoli & Isles in this friendship depression era cozy mystery series.

A NURSERY RHYME MYSTERY SERIES(mystery/sci fi)

Marlow finds himself teamed up with intelligent and savvy Sage Farrell, a girl so far out of his league he feels blinded in her presence - literally - damned glasses! Together they work to find the identity of @gingerbreadman. Can they stop the killer before he strikes again?

THE PERCEPTION TRILOGY (YA dystopian mystery)

Zoe Vanderveen is a GAP—a genetically altered person. She lives in the security of a walled city on prime water-front property alongside other equally beautiful people with extended life spans. Her brother Liam is missing. Noah Brody, a boy on the outside, is the only one who can help ~ but can she trust him?

Perception

Volition

Contrition

LIGHT & LOVE (sweet romance)

Set in the dazzling charm of Europe, follow Katja, Gabriella, Eva, Anna and Belle as they find strength, hope and love.

Sing me a Love Song

Your Love is Sweet

In Light of Us

Lying in Starlight

PLAYING WITH MATCHES (WW2 history/romance)

A sobering but hopeful journey about how one young German boy copes with the war and propaganda. Based on true events.

A Piece of Blue String (companion short story)

THE CLOCKWISE COLLECTION (YA time travel romance)

Casey Donovan has issues: hair, height and uncontrollable trips to the 19th century! And now this ~ she's accidentally taken Nate Mackenzie, the cutest boy in the school, back in time. Awkward.

Clockwise

Clockwiser

Like Clockwork

Counter Clockwise

Clockwork Crazy

Clocked (companion novella)

<u>Standalones</u>

Seaweed

Love, Tink

ABOUT THE AUTHORS

Lee Strauss is a USA TODAY bestselling author of The Ginger Gold Mysteries series, The Higgins & Hawke Mystery series, The Rosa Reed Mystery series (cozy historical mysteries), A Nursery Rhyme Mystery series (mystery suspense), The Perception series (young adult dystopian), The Light & Love series (sweet romance), The Clockwise Collection (YA time travel romance), and young adult historical fiction with over a million books read. She has titles published in German, Spanish and Korean, and a growing audio library.

When Lee's not writing or reading she likes to cycle, hike, and watch the ocean. She loves to drink caffè lattes and red wines in exotic places, and eat dark chocolate anywhere.

Norm Strauss is a singer-songwriter and performing artist who's seen the stage of The Voice of Germany. Cozy mystery writing is a new passion he shares with his wife Lee Strauss. Check out Norm's music page www.normstrauss.com

For more info on books by Lee Strauss and her social media links, visit leestraussbooks.com. To make sure you don't miss the next new release, be sure to sign up for her readers' list!

Did you know you can follow your favorite authors on Bookbub? If you subscribe to Bookbub — (and if you don't, why don't you? - They'll send you daily emails alerting you to sales and new releases on just the kind of books you like to read!) — follow me to make sure you don't miss the next Ginger Gold Mystery!

www.leestraussbooks.com
leestraussbooks@gmail.com

Printed in the USA
CPSIA information can be obtained
at www.ICGtesting.com
LVHW052007030823
754290LV00008B/162